ROCK HARD COWBOY

A Mile High Matched Novella

CHRISTINA HOVLAND

For rights information, please contact:
Prospect Agency
551 Valley Road, PMB 377
Upper Montclair, NJ 07043
(718) 788-3217

Holly Ingraham, Development Editor

First Edition, October 2018
Second Edition, February 2019

For my dad.

I miss you.

Chapter One
TWO WEEKS TO CHRISTMAS

Christmas sucked.

Also, Tucker McKay had great hair. Amazing black hair. Not too long. Not too short. The perfect length for running a girl's fingers through. And that little bit of a beard? It worked.

He was tall, dark and…never ever, ever.

On that thought, Mackenzie Bennett nursed her tall glass of seltzer water with a twist of lime while making herself seen in the newest hoity toity, excessively expensive Los Angeles nightclub. The fizzy bubbles in her drink had disappeared over an hour ago.

Music pulsed around her, the strobe lights on the dance floor below making the revelers appear as disjointed puppets. Funny that. If there was a disjointed puppet on the premises, it was her. Always doing what she was told. Always standing where directed. Always being someone else.

She kept a smile plastered on her face and her expression light. That's what a good actress did. Never show how you really feel when you're on the job. Always let the character shine through. In that moment, the character was the version of herself the public got to see. The smoky-eyed, shiny-haired starlet who really, deep down, wanted to spend her evening bingeing on Netflix while eating a grilled cheese sandwich created with the most over-processed American cheese product she could find.

God, she missed food like that.

She held her gaze on rocker-legend-slash-cowboy Tucker. The way he was propped up in a corner booth in the VIP section. The way his head bopped ever so slightly to the thump of the blaring music. The way his muscled arm was slung along the edge of the booth and his laughter permeated the VIP lounge.

"You're not having any fun." Her best friend and business manager, Leah, waggled a tipsy red-painted fingertip in her direction. Half her nails were red, half green. Very festive and all that.

"We're worried about you." Their not-quite-drunk friend Abby squeezed Kenzie's arm. "Do I need to call Taylor? Get the whole gang together?"

"We should do a holiday cheer intervention," Leah suggested. "We'll drink eggnog and make her sing 'Jingle Bells.'"

Kenzie couldn't help the smile that played at the corners of her mouth.

These women made up Kenzie's entourage. The ones who got the messy reality alongside the Hollywood glam. The ones who knew Kenzie had a secret passion for 1:00 a.m. bubble baths and writing screenplays that would never be produced. The ones who, no matter how adept an actress Kenzie was, would know she was putting up a front.

They knew her better than she knew herself most times.

So she didn't lie.

"I'm just doing my time." Kenzie nodded toward a group of women a level down on the dance floor. That group of ladies had been watching her for a solid twenty minutes.

One of the women waved back tentatively, giggled, and huddled with her friends.

"Your holiday spirit is seriously lacking." Leah snagged a martini from the waiter circulating a tray loaded with the drink of the day. Something orange and red—and it probably tasted like pineapple, if Kenzie had to guess.

"I'll find my Christmas cheer once the offer comes through." Kenzie eyed the sunset-colored drink. She wanted one, sure, but she wouldn't have one. Not when she was in public. Not when she was on a job. Even if the job was stupid. She was being paid an absurd amount of money to be at the club tonight. A club she had absolutely no intention of ever visiting again.

That wasn't the point though. Once she was seen somewhere, patrons would show up again and again, hoping to catch a glimpse of her. And since her last two box office receipts had been lacking, she filled in her budget gaps with appearances. Until the next opportunity moseyed along. Which would, she prayed to Lady Luck, be soon. Soon-ish.

"Any day. They'll come around any day now," Abby assured.

That was easy for her to say. Her life wasn't publicly and personally entwined in her ability to stay on the big screen. Sure, Kenzie had been smart with her money. Saved it. Invested it. But with the way Hollywood worked, her savings could only take her so far. She needed to nab a new role.

"Don't look back. The future is ahead." Leah made a dramatic hand motion like a soldier heading into battle.

Negotiations on Kenzie's latest movie—a romantic comedy about a farm girl in the big city—had fallen apart weeks ago, after her latest film flopped at the box office. Someone from the studio had leaked that they were eyeing other actresses for her part. Kenzie felt like the trap door had dropped open, spilling a washed-up actress just shy of stage left. It was all very, very public.

Very, very humiliating.

"I'm not looking back." No, she was looking straight at Tucker.

Kenzie's gaze slid the length of him. He might be a rock 'n' roll legend, but he was also muscled, charming, and a total jerk.

A jerk she'd shared a moment with at her premier last month. It was like in one of her movies, where the heroine sees the hero from across the room. They trace each other with their eyes, up then down, both liking what they see. And then something more—a connection—forms. Love at first sight? No, that doesn't happen. But definitely more than lust.

They'd chatted about the business, his music, her movies. He'd told her about his family, his ranch. She'd shared about her dreams of time away from the world, where she wouldn't always be the focus. Her job was her passion, but sometimes she dreamed of a break. Those were the times she'd doodle out a scene or two of her own creation. She'd told him that bit, too. Only those closest to her knew about her writing.

He was entirely too easy to talk to.

For a glimmer of a second, she'd thought what she and Tucker had between them was real. Not even the Hollywood brand of real, but out-of-the-spotlight *real*.

When she'd searched him out later that night to make a move, he was gone.

Then he told the press she was a crappy actress.

Then her movie lost a shit ton of money at the box office.

So, yeah, she was a little raw about it all.

That treatment from nearly anyone else? She'd merely smile and move along. She'd been in the business long enough to understand everyone had an opinion. But, for some reason, Tucker's mattered. His criticism stung. Tonight, she would remedy that. As soon as she figured out what to say.

"You should dance." Leah slipped her arm through Kenzie's and tugged her toward the VIP dance floor.

Abby linked her other arm and helped Leah scoot her along.

Not nearly as packed as the one downstairs, this dance floor was created for visibility throughout the club. Kenzie was being paid to attend tonight, and it was expected she appear to have a fabulous time.

Her contract said so.

"In a sec. I'm gonna talk to Tucker first." Kenzie disentangled her arms, stood tall on her stiletto heels, and weaved through the crowd toward him.

"That's a bad idea…" Leah continued talking but Kenzie ignored her.

What she was going to say? She had no idea. But she was going to tell him…something. Find out why he'd said mean things about her, what she'd done to offend him. That kind of thing. She'd figure it out.

Maybe something about how he'd hurt her feelings and he should apologize.

Yes, that's what she'd say. And she'd say it with style, and class.

The nearly transparent dress her stylist had outfitted her in made hustling anywhere practically impossible. The heels didn't help. So she took her time sauntering across the VIP section. Her bodyguard shadowed her movements. He was behind her, but she knew he was there. He was always there when she did these appearances.

"Tucker?" she asked, approaching his table.

His gaze lifted to hers. It softened for a split second. "Hey."

"I came by to say hello." She fidgeted with her glass. Which was unacceptable. She set it on the table and nudged it from the edge with her finger.

"Have a seat." He gestured to the other side of the booth. The guy sitting there scooted over to make room for her.

She didn't sit.

"I was thinking we could chat alone, about some of the things you mentioned to a reporter about my movie."

"Oh. That." He ran a hand over his neck. The movement made the defined muscles of his triceps bunch.

Dammit. She wasn't over here to check out his arms.

"Have your people call his people," one of his people said.

Kenzie leaned toward Tucker, ignoring his entourage. "I'd really like a conversation."

"Look." His eyes were soft again. He gave a nearly imperceptible shake of his head. "Magazines print what magazines print."

She took a deep breath.

"I just think—" Someone—a bulky someone—bumped her from behind.

The stilettos wobbled, her balance precarious. She threw her arm wide to catch herself. It didn't work.

Her knees buckled.

Damn. This was going to hurt.

She fell forward.

"Shit." Tucker moved to grab her.

Too late. The momentum caught her.

And that's how, two weeks before Christmas, she found herself face-first in Tucker McKay's crotch.

"NO." Absolutely not.

Tucker McKay might be willing to do a lot of things. Hell, he'd even put on a beat-up trucker hat because the damn stylist his record label assigned said it worked with his Justin cowboy boots. He may have once been the lead singer of a rock band, but he wasn't giving up his boots. Or his denim.

Especially for the leather pants and eyeliner they'd tried to force on him. That had been a hard no.

So, sure, he might do a lot of things, but not this. Not with her.

Even sellouts had limits.

And right now, his hard limit was being the arm candy of America's Hollywood Sweetheart—Mackenzie Bennett.

"You don't have a choice." His manager, Jessica, spread Kenzie's headshots across the shiny conference room table in the Los Angeles high-rise. He itched for his ranch in Colorado.

He glanced to the photos—as if he didn't already know what she looked like.

The pink-lipped mouth that launched a thousand wet dreams. The signature long red hair. The green eyes so bright they drew in millions of movie goers, and so sharp they'd shredded dozens of Hollywood hearts before tossing them aside like worn-out vinyl records.

Oh, he knew what she looked like, all right.

The clear twinkle lights on the Christmas tree in the corner flashed at him: *You're screwed. You're screwed. You're screwed.*

Then there were the photos of Kenzie's face dive into his pants three nights before. Someone had gotten a cell phone photo, and they'd wasted no time in selling it to the highest bidder. The gossip magazines went crazy with the image.

Tucker glanced to the closed door to ensure no one else played witness to Jessica's insanity. Just the two of them— figuring out how to extract him from the limelight without his last public image being Kenzie's head in his lap.

He'd started his career with a solid footing: refusing drugs, keeping his head down while he wrote music and performed for stadiums of screaming fans.

Then one day his muse walked out on him.

Everyone said there was a reason when you couldn't get the lyrics to flow. A bad breakup. Illness. You name it.

None of that had happened to him.

One day the pencil refused to work. The signature lyrics that had catapulted him to stardom wouldn't come. Boom. Done. *No more music making for you, Tucker. Oh, you have a career? Sorry, not sorry.*

Without new songs, there were no new records. He'd refused to spend the rest of his career rehashing the same old hits.

His band had imploded. Broken up. No more concerts, no more tours.

And for Tucker, no more music.

So he'd officially retired and was heading back to Colorado to run the ranch he'd bought years ago. He'd made an extraction plan that would allow him to return to music, if he ever desired. Not that he expected to be able to return, but Jessica convinced him not to close that door permanently. For the past six months, Tucker did what she'd said. Had been seen where she'd said to be seen. Dated who she'd said to date. And on the eve of his retreat back to Colorado, Kenzie faceplanted on his fly in the most public place possible.

Now, Jessica wanted America's Sweetheart to be his savior.

Most men would sell their left testicle to be Kenzie's arm candy.

He wasn't most men.

"Do you know what happened to Stefano Moretti?" Jessica asked, her tone all business.

Who the hell was Stefano Moretti? He gave Jessica his best, I-have-no-idea-what-the-hell-you're-talking-about look.

She clearly got the vibe. "Fashion icon. Daytime television star."

Still didn't ring a bell. He shook his head.

"Stefano had it all. Just like you. Then, as he was about to retire, he went to one of those outdoor Shakespeare theaters. The lady behind him accidentally spilled soda all over his head."

What in the actual hell was Jessica talking about?

"Photos were taken. The whole thing was plastered on all the covers of all the magazines," she continued.

What did a fashion model and a soda have to do with him?

"When you look up Stefano, you don't see the thousands of hours of work he put in on the catwalk. Or the daytime Emmy he won. You see photos of Stefano with soda in his hair." She paused, apparently for dramatic effect. "Kenzie with her face in your lap is precisely the same thing. You don't fix this? Change the dialogue? Change the images? Then when you're able to make music again, you'll have an uphill battle to fight, trying to get back into an industry that will only remember you as the guy with Mackenzie Bennett's face in your fly."

"When you put it like that…" He rolled his eyes toward the Christmas ornaments dangling on clear strings from the ceiling.

"Tucker." Jessica's expression firmed, even if the severe ponytail she always wore made certain there was no movement of the nearly non-existent creases of her forehead. "Deflecting the press is our only goal right now. A few public appearances with Ms. Bennett and you can both move on with your lives."

"I already moved on." If he spent too much time with Kenzie, he'd fall head over heart for her. He'd known it the first moment he'd seen her, and he couldn't take that risk. Not when he was leaving music. Not when he was packing it up and going back to the place where reality wasn't plastic.

The last thing he needed was to play with the fire that would burn them both.

Now he was here, in a conference room, starting it all again. "Fine. I'll do some dates. Pick someone else. Anyone."

"It's her, Tucker. A few very public appearances before Christmas is all we need to get the rumor mill rolling. By the new year, we'll announce you've decided to stay at your ranch in Colorado. The stress of the long-distance relationship will take its toll, and Mactuck will be over by the spring. You can continue on in whatever it is you plan to do, until you decide to come back."

Mac. Tuck. She couldn't be serious with this one. "You gave us a supercouple name."

It wasn't phrased as a question but rather a statement. Because, fuck it all, he knew she'd already tossed that bone to the two-dollar-rag magazines.

She raised an eyebrow. "Of course I did."

He used the trick he always used when he didn't like the way the conversation was going—he mimicked her expression. "And the best you could come up with is Mactuck?"

She sighed heavily. "It's very catchy. The press is already eating it up."

"Why does she get to be first? What about Tuckenzie." Okay, that sounded stupid even to his ears.

"No," Jessica said, deadpan.

He scraped a hand over the shadow of a beard he'd neglected to trim ever since Kenzie had faceplanted in his lap. Her crew had hustled her out of that club faster than he could process what had happened.

He couldn't sleep, had wanted to check on her. But checking would lead to feeling things. Feeling things would lead to doing things. Doing things would lead to him not following through on his retirement plan.

That couldn't happen. He needed out, before he became permanently entrenched in the façade of who he'd become in this place.

"She's on board with all of this?" The king of the rag magazines had quoted Tucker questioning her ability to play a character with any depth. It wasn't true—they'd twisted Tucker's words like they all did so well. But he hadn't corrected them, hadn't issued a statement that they'd messed up.

Because it was best if Kenzie just believed he was an asshole. It made keeping his distance a lot easier.

Still, the whole thing didn't sit well with him. It also didn't matter; an actress with the filmography of Mackenzie Bennett didn't care what he thought.

"Her camp already got her approval." He'd known when he started working with Jessica she was the best in the business.

"She knows you're officially retired," Jessica continued. "That you were on your way out. That her—what happened —put a serious wrench in your plans. And that now you need to fix it, as a team."

A light knock sounded from the conference room door.

The door slid open and Jessica's administrative assistant poked her head in. "Ms. Bennett and her manager are here."

"Hold up." Tucker held up a finger. "She's here?"

His skin started to flush in a way that was not okay. He was a lot of things—a musician who couldn't make music, a ranch owner who was never there, a cowboy playing the role of a rock star. He refused to be a star-crossed lover who started to sweat whenever a particular actress showed up.

"We're ready." Jessica pulled a chair out for Tucker. He crossed his arms. He'd stand. Thank you.

Jessica scowled in his direction.

And there she was. Kenzie. On the screen, she was larger than life. She took on whatever role she was playing so thoroughly, for years audiences had tripped over their feet to pay the box office fee. In person, she sucked all the air from the room—no need to announce her presence.

Or maybe that was just the reaction Tucker had to her.

"Tucker." She nodded to him, her usually kind-to-everyone eyes holding a frosty edge. Like one of those strawberry milkshakes from The Drive-In back home. Cold, smooth, and—sweet fuck, what the hell was he thinking?

"Mac"—he cleared whatever the hell had gotten stuck in his throat—"kenzie."

She slid onto one of the conference room chairs and flicked a glance to the Christmas tree in the corner. The frost melted, just a little.

Jessica's staff had gone all out with the tree. Huge-ass ornaments hung from oversized branches, the *you're-screwed* twinkle lights still flashed, and a buttload of wrapped boxes he'd bet his guitar were empty had been piled underneath. This was Hollywood after all—if there was one thing you could count on, it was that things were fake.

"Are you okay?" He focused on Kenzie. "From the fall?"

She glanced away. Unable—or unwilling—to meet his gaze.

Kenzie's manager shook her head and smacked a file folder on the table. "I'm Leah. Ms. Bennett is fine. We're not discussing the event at the nightclub."

"Of course. Everything is prepared. We're excited you've agreed to work with us." Jessica slid the contract toward Leah.

Standard confidentiality and all the other legal bullshit a pretend Hollywood relationship entailed.

"Perfect. We'll take a look and get it signed." Leah tucked the contract into the file folder.

"So..." Jessica went to sit, apparently changing her mind when Tucker didn't follow. At the moment, only Kenzie sat.

Fuck it.

He pulled out a chair, flipped it around and straddled it. "I've got a question."

Jessica glared a don't-mess-this-up stare in his direction.

"We all know what's in this deal for me. What's in it for you?"

Chapter Two
ELEVEN DAYS BEFORE CHRISTMAS

What was in it for her?

The headlines after her face-down tackle of Tucker's crotch said it all.

"Mackenzie Bennett on a Bender."

"Kenzie: Too Drunk to Dance?"

Her personal life was a paparazzi disaster splashed to hell and back across all mediums, from podcasts to national grocery store checkout-stand magazines. That would be enough to warrant a Hail Mary pass as Tucker's date du jour, but more than that, her professional life tilted on the precipice of obscurity. Even though she'd barely tipped the scales at thirty, by Hollywood's standards she was practically elderly. Toss in a couple of box office flops, and things were bad. When she showed up to a few red-carpet events nestled into the great Tucker McKay's side? Well, for a little while she would be relevant again.

So, what was in it for her?

"I'm a very giving person, and I understand you are in need of some assistance. I'm here to offer that assistance." That sounded so much better than the reality of the situation.

A little Hollywood-style filtering was all she needed to not sound like a pity case.

A slow grin spread across his lips. "You're phenomenal at bullshit."

Indeed, she was. Three of the highest industry award nominations—one win—said the same thing.

"Is that your way of saying I'm a decent actress?" She tilted her head to the side.

His smile faltered. His eyes went dark. He cleared his throat.

"Let's get to the details." His manager and the lead on his PR team piped in… What was her name? Jane. No. Janet. No. Jessica. Yes, Jessica.

"You can cut to the contract. I'm good with touching over clothes, kisses on the cheek, hand holding. That's it." Kenzie could be firm when she needed to be.

"No kissing on the mouth?" Jessica squinted at her.

The negotiations on these things were always a bitch.

Kenzie crossed her legs and then uncrossed them. "Do I have to?"

"It's more convincing that way."

Kissing Tucker wouldn't be a challenge. Fine. "No tongue."

"Done." Tucker smacked the table. His cheeks held only the slightest tint of pink to reveal his discomfort with the negotiations.

He was obviously not an actor. He should learn to control that.

"Jessica? Leah? Mind giving Mackenzie and me five minutes alone to go over specifics?" he asked.

Leah glanced to Kenzie for confirmation.

She nodded. There were a few things she'd like to say to Tucker, anyway.

"I'll wait in the hallway." Leah headed for the door, Jessica right behind her.

Tucker unfolded himself, so his full height dominated the room, and he caught the door for them, holding it wide like the gentleman he was not.

The heavy latch clicked closed. He leaned against it, staring at the carpet for two beats.

She waited him out.

His gaze raised to her. Oh damn. This was the Tucker she'd started to fall for, the Tucker she seemed to be powerless against. "I'm sorry."

Wait. "What?" she asked.

"I'm sorry. The magazine said I thought your movie was shit. I don't. I didn't."

"You didn't hate every bit of it while thinking I'm a— How did they word it?" She ticked her head toward the window and stared him down. "An actress who would best serve the world by selling fancy toasters on television at two a.m.?"

He filled his lungs with air and released it. Shook his head. Scratched at the bridge of his nose with the pad of his index finger. "No. I didn't say that."

"Their quote from you was oddly specific." She stood, pressing the palms of her hands onto the glass-topped conference table.

He kicked off from the door and strutted toward her. His cowboy boots weren't the polished kind. They were the worn in kind. The real kind. The sexy kind.

Ack.

She didn't need to be noticing the little things about him. This was a short-term deal they'd struck, there was no reason to care about his boots.

He rubbed at the side of his neck. "They twisted what I said."

The blood pressure she'd worked so hard to control over the past few days pulsed fast in her veins. "What exactly did you say about toasters? I'd like to know, given that I was included in the mix."

"Look, kissing movies aren't exactly my thing."

"Yeah? You're more of an exploding things kind of guy?" Sarcasm wasn't her forte, but she could make it happen on occasion.

He was close enough that she could see his pupils dilate. "I'm more of an I-don't-like-watching-the-girl-I've-got-a-thing-for-kiss-another-dickhead-on-a-magnified-screen kind of guy. That's why I told them the movie wasn't something I enjoyed. Where they got the toaster thing, I don't fucking know. Where do they get half their material?"

She paused. He felt a little of what she felt for him? "You have a thing for me?"

The look he gave her made her squirm.

"Because you like me?" she pushed.

"Mackenzie."

She wasn't letting this slide. Somewhere, deep down, she needed to know the way she'd felt wasn't so one-sided. "You like me?"

"Yeah."

They stared at each other a solid six seconds. Neither of them moved.

This couldn't go anywhere. The energy between them was intense, but she couldn't give him the power to hurt her again. Life was better without the reality of feelings. Keeping things on the surface meant it didn't matter when people said hurtful things.

"I do, Mackenzie."

She didn't break the invisible thread tying them together.

She had two choices in this scenario, and she leaned strongly toward the one in which she didn't open herself up again to betrayal. This business was all about taking care of number one. That was the game.

"That's too bad, but I accept your apology." She stood

and sauntered her best saunter toward the freedom of outside-of-this-room, then cast a quick glance over her shoulder. "Oh. Call me Kenzie. It's more believable that way."

Always Watch Out for Number One. That was her motto.

That and Never Get Too Close to the Guy Who Has the Power to Break Your Heart.

Chapter Three
SEVEN DAYS BEFORE CHRISTMAS

"You ready?" Tucker asked. They were attending the premier of some race car movie.

Kenzie was all Hollywood glitter today for their first red-carpet appearance. Her red hair had been curled and pinned so it managed to both be up and down at the same time. Even her dress sparkled. She looked stunning. "Absolutely."

He couldn't help but wonder what lay under all the glitter. All the shine. All the expected. She had a bite to her, that was for certain. His admission in the office and her subsequent dismissal was proof of that. Still, it didn't fit. She was a fantastic actress, but he'd caught a glimpse of something when he'd admitted his feelings for her. What? Well, who knew? In the moment, he'd thought it was reciprocation. She'd promptly blown that theory to hell.

Tucker angled himself so he could exit the limousine when they came to a stop. He'd go first, assist Kenzie and block the paps' view while she adjusted her dress. Take her arm. Smile and wave. Shake some hands as they passed the bleachers erected for the occasion.

Then the kiss.

Fuck. The kiss. Lips and all that shit.

The kiss would announce they were red-carpet official as a couple. Something Jessica had ensured brewed in the headlines over the past week.

It wasn't that he didn't want to kiss Kenzie. She was, after all, Mackenzie Bennett. So, yeah, on a primal level a lip-lock wouldn't suck. He just preferred not to tangle with a woman who so actively disliked him.

It was a personal choice.

"Should we have a secret abort-the-mission code?" he asked.

She raised an eyebrow at him like an expert. "Why would we need that?"

"In case we run into an ex on the red carpet? Get a reporter who asks too many questions? Decide we'd rather go have sushi?"

She shrugged, fidgeting with some of the silver rhinestones decorating her dress. "Once we step out of this car, pretty sure we'll pass the point of no return."

"Still, a word or a gesture might be good to let each other know we're in over our head."

"What do you propose we use?" They were creeping up to their spot. Not much time to decide at this point.

His phone rang in his pocket. He'd set it to silent—with one exception.

"Mom," he said, ducking his head slightly to the side.

"That nice reporter lady came by today."

Sonofabitch.

The paparazzi were *always* there. Partially because they wanted a good Tucker story, but mostly because his mother invited them in for her famous meatloaf. She loved the company, and they were more than willing to shoot the shit with her.

He growled inside. "I told you not to invite them inside."

"Psh. I didn't talk about you, no need to worry." He did worry, because he'd learned early on in his career that his mother, bless her soft heart, opened her mouth to reporters far too often. He made certain not to share any information about the sticky side of his career. Like the game of bait-the-paparazzi he was entangled in with Kenzie.

"They said you're seeing that Mackenzie Bennett." Her statement was entirely too innocent.

He hadn't mentioned the Kenzie situation to his mother. The last time she'd caught wind he was dating a movie star, she'd nearly flown out to Los Angeles to stalk his for-the-camera fake girlfriend.

"I'm headed to an event," he dodged. "I'll have to call you back when it's over."

"Oh, is she there? Right now? With you?" He could picture her perfectly. Sitting at the worn wooden kitchen table —she always sat there when she felt chatty and picked up the phone—the cell phone he and his siblings insisted she use pressed against her ear.

She was always "dressed to shoes," as she put it. Always ready for company—even if that company was a wild pack of reporters. "It's just nice to have visitors," she always said.

He called bullshit. She reveled in the attention.

His father? Not so much.

"Mom." A quick glance to Kenzie and his breath caught.

She'd clearly heard the whole thing, a wry smile tickling the corners of her mouth.

"You're bringing her home for Christmas, right?"

No, she wasn't coming home with him for Christmas.

First, because this whole thing was for show. And second, because his mother would be whipping out the baby bathtub photos before Tucker had a chance to pour a glass of spiced rum with his father.

"Everything okay?" Kenzie stage-whispered to him.

"Oh my God. That's her." His mother's *squee* was deafening. "She's right there. Tell her I loved her in *Wedding Confiden-*

tial. It's my favorite movie. Tell her I'll fix up the guest room for her when she comes to visit."

"I'm not doing this." He scowled out the window, the limousine creeping toward their destination in the line of other limousines.

"Well, she can't stay at your ranch. Not after what they said about her face in your lap. They'll twist it all around. Hand her the phone, sweetie," his mother prodded.

No way in hell.

"We're here. I'll have to call you back, Mom."

"She'll love Colorado. It's just like in that *Puppy Love* movie from a few years back. She was in it with that Gerald…oh, what's his name?"

"Hello, Mrs. McKay," Kenzie hollered from over his shoulder.

Dammit. Now he'd never hear the end of it.

"Bye, Mom." He clicked the phone off.

"Your mom seems sweet." Kenzie peered at him from beneath a sheet of long eyelashes.

"Sweet like a bobcat." He shook down the cuff of his white button-up shirt his stylist insisted he wear. God, he looked forward to dressing himself again. The lure of retirement was stronger and stronger.

The limo came to a stop at the beginning of the red carpet.

Kenzie fluffed her already perfect hair. A slight shift and the side of her gown parted at her thigh. All the saliva in his mouth disappeared. He swallowed sandpaper and glanced away.

He should think of something other than the milky skin of Kenzie's thigh.

Cattle.

He had cattle back home on his ranch in Colorado. Loads of cattle. If there was one thing that was not sexy in the least, it was doing a mental inventory of the heifers he knew by heart.

Less than eight days and he'd be back on the ranch. Back in a world where life made a helluva lot more sense than life under the spotlight of a concert stage and life on a red carpet pretending to be someone he wasn't.

His heart thumped against the wall of his chest.

Kenzie slipped her hand into his and squeezed. A little signal between the two of them. Like they were the real deal.

4

Chapter Four

Kenzie had her disinterested-yet-interested, charming-yet-aloof, red-carpet walk down to an art.

Step out of the limo. Take Tucker's arm. Saunter. Saunter. Strut. Saunter. Smile. Laugh. Hand on hip. Turn so all the photographers have an equal chance at selling to the cover of *In Time*. Repeat. Ad infinitum.

A million camera shutters seemed to snap around them like a herd of angry click beetles. That's what she and Leah called the paps, especially when they twisted things so far even the punctuation of their stories spread their lies.

Tucker's hand rested at the open back of her gown, his fingertips heating her skin.

This was it. Red-carpet official.

She would not fall.

A glance at him and his eyes warmed—mostly they were blue, but just around the pupil they turned the color of Dom Pérignon Brut Champagne. They were eyes a girl could get drunk on. He raised his eyebrows as a nearly imperceptible question.

The kiss. They were supposed to do that. Now.

Smile perma-fixed to her lacquered lips, she raised her palm to his cheek and lifted onto her toes so she could press her mouth to his.

As planned, he opened for her, making a good show of it.

That was all this was. A really good show.

Except, at the touch of her lips to his, her insides twisted around themselves. Like the first time she'd set foot at one of her premiers—she'd been twelve and had known instantly that fame was her drug of choice. Right now, she'd trade all of that for more of this. More Tucker. To taste every inch of him. To feel every part.

Damn, she was a good actress. She'd even convinced herself she had feelings for him.

As expected, the paparazzi went bananas.

"Ms. Bennett, when did you and Mr. McKay—"

"How long have you two been to—"

Tucker pulled away. His breath played against her ear. "See, they have no memory of the nightclub."

One of the click beetles shouted, "Kenzie, is this because you fell in his—"

She turned to Tucker, gave him a they-never-forget look, and mentally checked that her perma-smile remained in place.

"Tucker, will you still be going to Colorado for the holidays?" someone shouted.

Tucker squeezed Kenzie's hand. "Absolutely."

"Will Ms. Bennett be going with you?" another shouted.

"We haven't decided," Tucker replied.

If there was one thing Kenzie had learned in all her time in front of the cameras—don't give firm answers. Vague was the name of the game. Unless you wanted reporters to show up somewhere, but she was pretty sure Tucker didn't want them to descend on his ranch.

Tucker obviously knew the name of the game, too. He squeezed her hip.

She refused to acknowledge the butterflies that flitted around inside at his touch.

They made it to the entry of the theater, the heels of her Louboutins sinking into the plush carpet. The buzz of the other A-listers hummed throughout the room for the party before the screening.

"I'm gonna grab a beer." Tucker jerked his chin toward the bar set up in one corner. "Get you anything?"

"Club soda?" She'd already shared with him that she didn't drink in public. Bad things happened when she wasn't on her game. Bad things, like…well, what had happened two weeks earlier.

"Done." The thing about Tucker was he didn't have dimples in the traditional sense. Instead, he had one little dimple just under his left eye, high on his cheek when he smiled. Girls all over the word adored that little patch of skin. Kenzie was no different. And when he sang, and it popped? Sweet angel of Audrey Hepburn, she'd go on a Roman Holiday with him anytime.

Which was why he needed to scoot along and grab her some carbonated water.

He didn't just remove his palm from the skin of her back, no, he slid it along the line of her dress, leaving a path of goosebumps.

Then he disappeared into the swirling mass of California's elite.

"Mackenzie."

Everything paused. She knew that voice. It was the voice of producer Eileen "the snake" Hendrix. Kenzie and Leah had been waiting to hear from Eileen for weeks about the lead role in *Wander Love*. Eileen had the power to squelch Kenzie's career—or make it soar again.

Kenzie angled herself toward the woman in charge of her destiny. "Eileen. So lovely you're here."

"A word?" Eileen asked.

Kenzie followed Eileen to the side of the room opposite from Tucker. The soundproofing carpet along the wall brushed her arm.

"What can I do for you?" *Why haven't you returned my calls?* Kenzie asked silently, hopeful the quirk of her eyebrow would relay the unspoken question.

"You and Tucker are an item now?" Eileen asked, quietly enough so only Kenzie could hear, but not quite a whisper.

Kenzie nodded, her gaze flicking to the man in question. "Something like that."

"I hate to put you on the spot," Eileen said in a way that implied she had no problem doing it. "The thing is"—deep sigh—"we've been trying to convince him to do the title song for *Wander Love*."

Eileen took the tiniest sip of her champagne and stared into the crowd. The studio was rumored to be sparing no expense on the flick. In La La Land, that meant big things for an actress in the starring role.

"Tucker's retired. I'm certain you've heard." With the explosive breakup of his band, everyone capable of breathing in the continental United States had heard about it.

Eileen nodded in fake agreement. "That's the thing though. I'm curious how serious he is about retirement right now."

"Pretty serious, I think." Given the whole charade they were tied up in as part of... What was it his manager had called it? An extraction plan.

"I don't suppose you might talk to him about his refusal. Convince him to postpone his retirement until after he pens something for *Wander Love*?" Eileen had a way of saying things that somehow managed to be a question and a command at the same time.

Kenzie refused to squirm. "I'm not sure I have any power over Tucker's decisions."

"Come on, dear. I think when one is inspired enough, they can move mountains." Eileen's innuendo was clearer than a Colorado sky, but Kenzie didn't play that game. Never, she'd *never* sold herself for a part. No way would she start now. Still though, she could convince Tucker without bedroom tricks, if that was the leverage it would take to get her career back on track.

Dammit.

"To confirm," she asked. "If Tucker does the song, then the part is mine? With fees to match the last project I did with your studio?"

Eileen scoffed at the direct hit. She eyed Kenzie. "Yes."

Kenzie glanced around, her gaze landing on Tucker talking to some guy wearing ripped jeans at a red-carpet event. Now that took some balls. "How long do I have to convince him?"

"Until the new year?" Eileen sipped again. "We really need to shore up our lead actress, you know?"

Oh, yes. Kenzie knew, all right.

"He'll do it," she heard herself say.

Only she had no idea how she'd convince him.

"I'm so pleased to hear that." Eileen practically flicked a forked tongue into the air between them, searching for weakness.

"Leah and I will need some reassurance that once he does, the part is mine." Always Watch Out for Number One.

"Consider it done. Have Leah contact my office on Monday." Eileen slithered away, back into the abyss.

Kenzie escaped to the nearest bathroom—the private kind often used for hookups or, in her case, a private conversation. Cell to her ear, she practiced deep breathing until Leah picked up.

"Do you need a rescue?" Leah asked as a hello.

"No." Kenzie dropped to the cushy chair by the stack of

rolled hand towels. "I need to figure out how to convince Tucker to do a song for Eileen's movie."

She relayed the conversation.

Leah paused a moment. "So, you're not out. This is good. Talk to Tucker. See what he says."

"He's already told her he won't do it."

"How do we get that no to turn into a yes?" Leah asked.

Kenzie blew a breath that made her bangs fly straight up. "I have no idea."

"Maybe start by just asking him?" Logic wasn't so stupid in this case.

"I can do that." Kenzie stood, adjusted her dress. She could ask. See what he said. Maybe he would do it.

"Don't be too direct though. Try to make it seem like it's his idea. Guys love that."

Kenzie rolled her eyes. "I'll work on it."

She tucked her cell back into her black Prada clutch with the silver clasp. It shouldn't be too hard to convince a man set on retirement to do one last song.

One last song, for her.

"RETIREMENT, HUH?" Tucker's buddy Brek asked.

Brek managed Dimefront, the current "it" band. Especially since Tucker's band had broken up at his announcement of retirement.

Brek didn't get wrapped up in the bullshit of the industry. That was why he and Tucker could be friends. No pretention between them, just beer and solid love of music.

"Yup. Done with all this." Tucker gestured to the crowd with the brown bottle of craft beer in his hand, Kenzie's seltzer in the other. He'd prefer a draft beer in a mug in the bar back at home. At events like this? Beggars couldn't be choosers. "It's been time for a while."

His band had gone their separate ways. Tucker wasn't making music anymore. Not that the industry believed it. Labels continually tossed offers his way. He wished he could take them—but taking them involved actually being able to create something.

Reality and his ranch looked better and better.

Jessica was right, though, the last thing he wanted was to have the final memory of his time in the limelight be that photo of Kenzie sprawled over his lap at a night club. So, he'd water down the image. Make a few more appearances. Give the rags something to talk about.

Then he'd go home.

Tucker scoured the room for Kenzie. She'd disappeared. "You should come see the ranch."

"I'd like that." Brek took a pull of his own beer.

"Tucker?" Kenzie sidled up next to him. Where the hell had she materialized from? "Sorry. Had to make a call."

His gaze hooked on her and his lungs ached. He could still taste her on his lips. Her toes barely peeked out from under the long ball gown she wore. Hell, even her dress kissed the ground she walked on.

"Everything okay?" Tucker handed her drink to her.

Her red curls bobbed as she nodded. "Yup."

"This is my buddy Brek. Brek, Kenzie."

"Hi." Kenzie took the drink, she nodded toward his friend and her expression warmed. "It's nice to meet Tucker's friends."

Brek's forehead crinkled as she shook his hand. "The other half of Mactuck. In the flesh," he said.

Tucker groaned on the inside. Mostly. Some slipped out, he couldn't help it.

"Headed home for Christmas?" Tucker asked, distracting Brek from any further discussion of their supercouple nickname.

Brek's eyes lit up in response, like he knew exactly what

Tucker was doing. "I'm headed back to Denver. Aspen's pregnant."

Aspen… Tucker ran through his mental Rolodex. Brek's sister.

"Uncle Brek, yeah?" Tucker was an uncle three times over. He looked forward to playing up that role, now that he wasn't tied to a tour schedule.

"Has a nice ring." Brek shot a look toward Kenzie. "Big plans for the holidays?"

"A quiet holiday for me." Kenzie was the queen of being vague when she needed to be. Tucker had noted her ability to say something and nothing at the same time. "We do Vail every year. My mother has a big bash. Maybe I'll crash Tucker's family party and we can go skiing." She winked at him.

Dammit, he liked it when she flirted with him. His internal alarm bells started dinging.

Kenzie plus Colorado plus his family was a horrible idea. His mother would go crazier with decorations than normal. They'd be the green and red kind where nothing matched, but everything somehow worked. Not like Hollywood decorations, where everything was silver and gold and positioned for maximum effect.

"I like her, Tuck." Brek raised his beer bottle in salute. "Let's touch base after the new year. Plan something. I should go check on the boys, make sure they're not fucking shit up."

Tucker nodded. "Good call."

He and Kenzie stood there, not saying anything. She shifted. He shifted. She tucked her wallet thing under her arm. He stared at the carpet.

"So, hey. We're here." Kenzie seemed to study the bubbles in her drink like they were a movie reel spinning an especially good story.

He tilted her chin up, his fingertip resting in the soft skin under her jaw. "Hey."

The voices in the room seemed to drift aside. They shared the moment, and it was all that mattered.

"I wasn't serious about the skiing thing. I wouldn't barge into a family Christmas." She lifted her drink's straw to her lips. Closed them around the tip. Took a long drink.

Sonofabitch, he'd never been jealous of a straw before.

"So, Eileen was mentioning that they'd like you to do the music for one of her movies. Have you talked to her about it?" Kenzie broke the spell.

He dropped his hand. "What?"

"Eileen, you know…" Kenzie waved to the producer who'd been hounding him for months about a movie that needed a theme song.

Yeah, he knew Eileen. Relentless Eileen.

"I already told her no." And why did Kenzie care, anyway?

She fidgeted with her straw. "You know this town. Saying no to a project just means they haven't offered you enough money."

Not in his case. Saying no was because he couldn't deliver, and even if he could, he wouldn't do a project for Eileen. Just the thought made him shiver. She sucked the life out of anyone in the room. "Retirement usually means a person stops working in the field."

"Except in Hollywood. You should add that to the end of your statement." She clearly was trying to make things light.

"In my case, retirement means I've got two hundred head of cattle ready for my attention."

Her expression turned confused. "I don't get it. Is that a joke?"

He scratched behind his ear. "Ah, no."

"Oh my God, you're serious." She gripped his shoulder with her free hand. "I know you said you're going home. You're really giving up on music to raise…beef?"

A slow smile spread through him. That was exactly what he was doing. "Yeah."

"Holy crap." She studied him as if *he* was a piece of beef.

He found attentive Kenzie entirely too attractive. The way he was feeling toward her was not light.

And that was unacceptable.

Chapter Five
FIVE DAYS BEFORE CHRISTMAS

Tucker had survived the rest of the night with Kenzie. They'd played their respective parts like band members who could predict each other without even a word.

That was two days ago. Today they were going to have lunch at The Ivy. Jessica and Leah had picked the location to be sure Tucker and Kenzie were seen by the right photographers.

He sat up, giving up on sleep. The blanket he'd tossed across his lap last night bunched at his waist. He'd shipped his bed back to Colorado weeks ago. As a certified rocker, sleeping on the couch shouldn't have been playing such havoc on his back. How many nights had he passed out on a random sofa in a random penthouse?

His spine cracked and twinged in response.

He wanted his damn bed back.

What he really needed was to be at his ranch, not surrounded by the corrugated cardboard boxes he'd started packing weeks ago. He'd kept the bare minimum in his high-rise Los Angeles apartment. Usually, he put up at least a tree for Christmas. Not this year.

A slow inventory of the few items left in his studio apartment: his guitar, sofa, kitchen shit. He wouldn't miss the floor-to-ceiling windows—not when his ranch had the same thing, with a view he preferred. Wouldn't miss access to every possible thing a guy could want within walking distance—not when his ranch had everything he needed. And he sure as hell wouldn't miss sharing so much space with so many other people—not when he'd be living in a town with a population of 693. Soon to be 694.

His phone buzzed from the coffee table. He grabbed it, checked it, clicked the green call button, and held it to his ear.

"Dad." He sat to attention. His father never called. That duty was delegated to his mother.

"I just fixed your mother a kale smoothie." His father's ranch-hardened voice sounded like he'd gulped a mouthful of gravel. "It's green."

Tucker scrubbed a hand over his face. "Do I want to know why you're making Mom smoothies?"

"Because she and Betsy started a running club. It's icy at the buttcrack of dawn." A pause. "Both of 'em fell on the ice. Twisted the shit out of her ankle."

Tucker's stomach began the slow sinking he knew wouldn't end well. His mother didn't run. She didn't drink healthy stuff. And she didn't have his father call when she could do it herself. "Why the hell is she running and drinking kale?"

"Saw you on the television. Then the reporters started calling." There it was. Damn. She'd been chatting with the reporters. "She got wind you're bringing home that actress."

That actress. He couldn't help the film running through his thoughts. The way Kenzie had looked in that dress. The way her mouth had fit so perfectly against his. The way she'd tasted like peach lip gloss. "I'm not—"

"Son." His dad paused. Tucker could almost see him pinching the bridge of his nose. Not willing to tell his wife no.

But also not buying into the drippings that came along with Tucker's fame.

"Dad, I'm not bringing her home. We don't give specifics about our plans because, if we do, there's a camera shoved in our face everywhere we go."

"I don't get involved in your life. But your mother hasn't been this excited about anything in a long while. You ran off to sing your songs, we supported you. I've never asked for anything from your career. But if you can get that actress to come visit her, you'll have made her decade."

No. Nuh-uh. No way. Bringing Kenzie home to the folks was the opposite of keeping it light. "Dad—"

"First thing tomorrow, I'm driving an hour to town to stock up on more goddamned kale. Swear to heaven, you don't bring that girl to meet your mother, and I bought all this green shit for nothing, there will be tears on Christmas. Do you want tears on Christmas?"

Tucker did not want tears on Christmas. He also had no claim on Kenzie or her Christmas whereabouts.

"I don't expect we'll be together much longer."

"Well, that would break your mama's heart."

"I figured you'd want me and Kenzie to break up so you can stop making vegetable drinks."

"Seeing how your mama's eyes light at the possibility of you bringing her home? Well, I'll feed her all the vegetable juice she wants."

This was bad.

"You know these things aren't what they seem." He couldn't tell his mom, but his dad wouldn't snitch. He could lay it all out to get off the hook.

His father ignored him. "Broke her heart not to see you but twice a year for so long."

A lump of regret caught in his throat. His dad knew his buttons, that was for sure. He hadn't meant to make his mother sad. Never meant to stay away so long. Traveling, gigs, it all added up over time.

He'd do anything to make it up. His mind drifted to how Kenzie would look sitting at his mother's table.

No.

He'd do *almost* anything

"Don't ruin her Christmas," his father commanded.

The line went dead.

Dammit. How the hell was he going to convince Mackenzie Bennett to come home with him to small-town Collbran, Colorado at Christmastime?

KENZIE'S BEL AIR bungalow was tucked off the main road. He pulled up to the gate and pushed the button on the speaker box.

"Tucker McKay for Mackenzie Bennett."

He waited while whoever managed her security did their thing and checked him out.

A click and the gate swung open.

Tucker drove up the windy drive, his Jeep Cherokee hugging the asphalt curves. He climbed out and his boots clopped along the concrete steps up to the huge archway, practically announcing he was now in the lair of America's Sweetheart.

He barely had his fingertip on the bell when the door swung open.

"Well, Tucker McKay. Imagine that."

He'd heard of her. Moira Bennett. The original momager. The Kardashians had nothing on her drive and persistence.

Kenzie had replaced her a few years back, and Moira was not happy. Word was they'd had a falling out over the whole thing. Color him shocked to see her in Kenzie's home. Then again, he was proof some would do anything for family.

"Tucker?" Kenzie stood at the top of the arched marble stairway, her eyebrows puckered together. Without changing the expression on her beautiful face, she clipped down the stairs toward him in her stilettos.

Fuck, she even wore stilettos at home. Small-town Colorado was going to eat her alive. It wasn't like he was asking her to visit Telluride or Aspen—places where her stiletto-ed feet would fit right in with the eclectic fashion and five-hundred-dollar steaks. No, he wanted to take her to a muddy ranch to meet his now-kale-drinking mother in the sticks.

"You're early." Kenzie's statement was more of an accusation, and the way she wouldn't meet her mother's eyes told him exactly why.

"I've been looking forward to meeting you, Tucker. Kenzie's told me so much about you." Moira held out her hand to him.

He shook it.

Fuck, even the woman's hand was cold.

Kenzie had the look of a twelve-point buck in the headlights of his Silverado back home. "My mom was just heading out."

Moira squeezed his fingers a few extra unnecessary seconds. "But I don't mind sticking around to say hello."

Kenzie's expression hardened. "Nope. Time to go."

"Well, I look forward to seeing you at my Christmas party then, dear." Moira gave her a stare with more sharp edges than a set of steak knives. "Tucker?" She turned her stare to him, the steak knives dissolving on contact. "Do you have plans for the holidays? We'd love to have you attend. Vail is wonderful this time of year."

No way in hell.

"Headed home, ma'am. Won't be able to make it." He turned on the charm, held her gaze, nodded just a bit—a trick he'd learned on the road to make a rejection not feel so personal.

Kenzie pulled open the heavy wooden door. "Thanks for stopping by, Mom. Talk soon."

Her mother sailed across the threshold, pausing only briefly to kiss Kenzie's cheek.

The door pushed closed, and Kenzie leaned against it, her breaths measured.

"Are you o—"

She held up a finger. "Give me a second."

He waited.

"What're you doing?" he finally asked.

"Trying to figure out how to get out of going to my mother's for Christmas." Head raised, she pasted on a smile he knew wasn't honest. "Okay, what's up?"

He shoved his hands in the pockets of his jeans. "I believe I may have a solution to your problem."

"You found out I was switched at birth?" she asked, totally serious.

"No, I have a proposition for Christmas."

"After the argument I had with my mother just now, I really hope you're not screwing with me."

"I thought you might enjoy spending some time with my family at Christmas. Come visit the ranch." There it was. All laid out for her like a picnic.

She stilled. "I thought we agreed to keep things light. Meeting your family for a major holiday isn't light."

A shrug, they could spend the holidays together and still keep things light, if that was what she wanted. "It'll give the reporters something to print."

She pressed her hands against her waist. "That's not it. What're you angling at here, Tucker."

He sighed. She could read him like a pro. "It seems our mothers had the same idea. Mine wants me to invite you to the ranch for Christmas. Dad's being persistent about it, and I figured I had to at least ask."

"Your family wants me to come and do an appearance,"

she hedged. "It's not that you want me to come."

He gritted his teeth. He wanted her to come. He wanted her to be in his house. He wouldn't kick her out of his bed, either. That was the damn problem. "My family wants to meet you, and I want you to come."

"Why?"

"What do you mean, why?"

"Why do *you* want me to come?" She spoke slowly, as though talking to a toddler.

"Because I'm inviting you?" Wasn't that enough? He wouldn't invite her, no matter how manipulative his mother was being, if he didn't, deep down, want her there with him.

And he wasn't going to dive any further into that line of thought. His goal was to get out of Los Angeles, not fall for the ringleader.

"Tucker."

He scrubbed a hand over his cheek. She wasn't going to make this easy.

"Yeah," he replied.

"Is it too much for you to admit that you're asking a friend for a favor with your family?"

When she put it like that… "No."

"Then you should say it. Like it really is." She made a little "come on" motion.

"You know that's what I meant."

She crossed her arms over her chest.

Apparently, they were doing this. "I like you. You know that part."

"Keep going." More of the "come on" motion.

"We get along."

"Not so hard, is it?" She made the motion again.

"And I'd like to ask my friend, that'd be you, for a favor."

"I love doing favors for friends. What is it that you need?" Her hands dropped to her hips.

"Would you make my mother's Christmas wish come true and visit her?"

Kenzie's eyes sparkled like the *you're-screwed* twinkle lights in Jessica's office. "When do we leave?"

"Christmas Eve?"

"Perfect."

"Not so fast. Now it's your turn." He held up his hand, extended and curved his index finger in his own "come on" motion.

She raised one eyebrow. The muscle control in her forehead was really quite impressive. "My turn for what?"

"Way I see it, I've admitted twice that I like you."

"Okay." She dropped her arms and started to go past him to the threshold. "Good talk we've had here."

He stepped in front of her, his hands shoved in his pockets so he wouldn't reach out and touch what wasn't his. "It's your turn."

She returned her hands to her hips. "To tell you I like you?"

"Yes."

"What if I don't?"

"Then you probably shouldn't come home with me."

She pressed her lips together. "I like you, Tucker."

"Do you have a thing for me like I have a thing for you?" Might as well know up front, before they spent a week at his ranch.

"I thought we agreed we're not doing that." She said it, but she didn't sound committed.

He shook his head. "No, you said that. I didn't actually agree."

"Well, I tell you what." She sauntered toward him like the movie star she was. "Let's go to Colorado and maybe you'll find out."

Then she lifted herself to her toes, and without an audience, Mackenzie Bennett kissed him, pressed herself along the length of his body, drank him in. He parted his lips, and the tip of her tongue touched his in exploration. He responded with a moan. He couldn't help it. Didn't want to try.

Kenzie had her lips pressed to his, her tongue in his mouth, and she smiled. Smiled like she had just won the prize. What the prize was, he had no idea. And he didn't care. He slipped both hands into her hair, tilting his head to deepen the kiss further. This time, she made a deep noise in the back of her throat. It was his turn to grin. The palms of her hands slid up and over the muscles of his back to his neck.

As quick as it'd started, Kenzie released him. She grabbed her bag from the table by the door and stepped outside.

As though nothing had happened at all.

Chapter Six
THREE DAYS BEFORE CHRISTMAS

Kenzie took Tucker's hand as they made their way up the front steps to her friend Taylor's house. Her stomach took a little tumble when Tucker's thumb traced her knuckles.

She couldn't believe she'd kissed him before their public lunch the other day. She also couldn't get it out of her head. That and the fact that she'd agreed to go home with him for Christmas. Kenzie wasn't the kind of woman a guy brought home to his mother. Case in point? She'd never been brought home to anyone's mom.

They stepped through the doorway to a party in full swing. A jazz band played Christmas carols while waiters carried trays of champagne flutes through the black-tie event.

Taylor was a television executive and her home reflected the woman people thought she was—straight lines, severe angles, and a multitude of gray hues. Her friends knew that was all a front and deep down she was pure marshmallow fluff. For Taylor's annual Christmas soirée, some decorator had added silver to all the gray. Even the Christmas tree was silver —an abstract art piece made of thousands of little mirrors.

Tucker dropped Kenzie's hand and placed his palm

against her back, tethering her to his side. She ignored how his touch warmed her. Well, tried to ignore it. Her body wasn't having any of that.

"What do you say we have dinner after?" Tucker leaned close, so she could feel his breath against her earlobe.

Kenzie's stomach rumbled in agreement. "Can't. I've got to pack for our trip to Colorado."

They left in two days. Truth was, her stylist had already packed for her, but Kenzie needed some time for herself after events like this. Time away from who she was *supposed* to be, so she could *just* be Kenzie. Binge on Netflix and exist in a bubble that didn't involve anyone but her.

"Thank God you're here." Taylor hurried toward them in a silver sequined gown that matched the house. "I'm going to borrow Kenzie for just a moment."

"Of course." Tucker dropped his hand.

She immediately missed it.

"Food's that way." Taylor gestured toward the spread in her dining room.

Tucker nodded, winked at Kenzie, and headed toward a cluster of guests near the table.

"What's up?" Kenzie followed Taylor through the crowd toward the patio.

"Okay. Well." Taylor's cheeks were flushed. "You know the writing you've been doing? The story in Paris? I mentioned it to a friend."

Kenzie's blood seemed to thin. Her pulse seemed quicker. Colder.

"What friend?"

"Alex."

Shit. Shit. Shit.

Alex wasn't just a friend. He was the man behind the curtain for most of the movies on Flicker, the latest streaming channel.

"And he loved it," Taylor continued. "Wanted to know when he can read it."

Kenzie wasn't a writer. She was an actress who wrote things down. Occasionally. Nothing serious.

"He can't." Kenzie crossed her arms over her chest. "Those screenplays are private. I shared them with you as a friend. Not so you can shop the ideas around."

"They're good, Kenz. You need to think about letting someone other than your cat read them."

"I don't have a cat."

"Then my point is even more valid." Taylor raised her eyebrows.

"Taylor?" Her date of the night, a record executive, asked from the doorway. "There's something going on with the caterer. You need to come see this."

"Be right there." Taylor turned to him and gave a little wave. Then she looked to Kenzie. "Consider it. Seriously."

Kenzie braced her arms on the railing when Taylor went back to her guests. She had a good heart, but she shouldn't have shared Kenzie's idea. It wasn't her place.

"Everything okay?" Tucker's voice slid over her.

She turned toward him.

He stood in the doorway, his tuxedo backlit from the glitz of the party. He'd even polished his cowboy boots for the night. Tucker looked more delicious than the champagne circling on silver trays in the room behind him.

Thousands of little bubbles sizzled through her bloodstream at the sight of him.

One look at her and his expression slipped to concern.

"Everything's not okay," he confirmed as he stepped to her, ran a hand over her arm. "What happened?"

He already knew that she wrote, from the first time they'd met. She'd opened up to him and it had come up. He also knew she didn't talk about it much. So, his understanding that she wasn't thrilled Taylor had chatted it up with an industry executive wasn't a surprise.

"Your friend was just trying to help. I'm certain." He stood close to her. His hands resting at her elbows, soothing her. "She didn't give him the pages. What is it that's truly bothering you?"

Kenzie glanced up at him, catching his gaze from under her eyelash extensions. "What if it's not good? The writing."

What if she embarrassed herself? A flop with a script she hadn't written was one thing. One that was her baby was a whole different game.

The pad of his thumb traced her jawline. "Let me read it."

"You?"

"An honest, unbiased outsider who knows a little about putting words together." The edge of his mouth quivered with humor.

She couldn't help it, he cupped her cheek and she let him. "You're being serious about this."

"One hundred percent." His thumb traced the edges of her lips, the motion echoing intimately further below.

"Why do you want to help me?" she asked, gripping the sleeves of his tuxedo.

"Sometimes people do things for other people because they want to, not because there's something in it for them."

That wasn't true in the world they lived in.

She opened her mouth to respond, but before she could say anything, Tucker brushed his lips against hers.

And she lost herself to another Tucker kiss. Firm, hot, and all Tucker.

"Are you ready to reconsider dinner?" he asked when their lips separated. "We've been seen. I'm all dressed up. You're all dressed up."

Normally, Kenzie wanted to be by herself after an event, but tonight some time with Tucker sounded...nice.

"How about we order in? Watch some TV?" she asked. "Change into something not black-tie?" She gestured between them.

His hand found hers. "I couldn't think of a better way to spend the evening."

IN THE LOTTERY OF LIFE, Tucker had won. At least for the night. Merry Christmas and all that.

This was his thought as *Arrested Development* played over Kenzie's eighty-five-inch flat screen while they lounged on her sofa, her back to his front. His arm draped over her waist. He still wore his dress pants but had ditched the jacket and bow tie and had undone the top buttons on the shirt.

Kenzie toyed with his hand while the television flashed. She had changed into yoga pants that did amazing things for her assets and a top that fell off her right shoulder. He wanted to run his lips over her skin there, but he didn't. Kenzie clearly needed some time in her own head. But she'd invited him in, and he'd taken the offer. He'd give her the time she needed without heating things up.

Kenzie snuggled deeper into his embrace. "Thank you."

"For what?" he asked.

"For just chilling with me."

"It's not a hardship." He shifted as she turned so they were face-to-face. Her leg slipped between his and he couldn't do this anymore.

The chilling part.

He rolled Kenzie to her back. "I'm sorry."

She laughed. "For what?"

Then he met her mouth with his and ran his hands up under her shirt to the cloth of her bra. "For not chilling."

Kenzie got his intent—not that it was hidden—and met

his kiss with her own. His tongue with her own. Her hand slid over his ass, his slid under her bra to the skin there.

Yes, the lottery of life had been pretty damn awesome. He may not have a career anymore, but at least he had Kenzie and a couch.

"I can live with not chilling." Kenzie said, her hands wandering under his waistband to the fly of his pants, working the button free. "Chilling is so overrated."

She worked his zipper lower, nipped his bottom lip, and ground herself against his thigh. How she did all those things at once? He had no idea, but he appreciated her dedication to not chilling together.

"Kenzie?" a female voice called from somewhere in the hallway.

Tucker and Kenzie froze.

"Shit." Kenzie scooted from beneath him. "Hang on," she yelled back. "It's Leah."

"Your manager?"

"My best friend." She righted her shirt from where he'd been pawing at her.

"Ah." Tucker leaned back on his knees.

"Seriously, Leah. Stay there. Be right there," Kenzie hollered. Her hands met Tucker's in an attempt to get him zipped and buttoned back up. "She can't find you here like this. I'll never live this down."

"Oh my God, what are you doing with Tucker?" Leah yelled back.

"Seriously. Just. A. Second." Kenzie fumbled with Tucker's fly, her cheeks pink, her breaths uneven. Generally, that was the reaction when the fly was undone, not being put back together.

"Why won't this zipper zip?" Kenzie fought with the zipper in question.

This could end very poorly.

He caught her wrists and held them to his lips. Kissed

them one at a time. "I'll do that part. Why don't you go meet your friend."

She dropped her face to her hands. "I'm so sorry."

He traced her cheekbones with his thumbs. "Don't be. Is there a back door?"

Kenzie deflated. "She's already seen your Jeep out front."

"Then let's own this." Tucker tilted her chin and brushed his lips against hers.

"'Kay," Kenzie said on a breath.

"I'll say hello and then I'm gonna head out, but you owe me an e-mail," he continued.

"Wha—"

He placed his finger to her mouth. "Your screenplay. I'll read it before we leave town."

Kenzie's expression softened. "'Kay."

At least he'd have something to do for the rest of the night to get his mind off of everything that hadn't happened. Merry Christmas and all that.

Chapter Seven
CHRISTMAS EVE

The baggage carousel sat unmoving in the small airport. Tucker said they were an hour away from his ranch. Kenzie dropped to a brown pleather chair at the luggage claim. She'd tucked most of her hair into a baseball cap, so only a few wisps of her distinctive red fell to her shoulders. Minimal makeup and a big puffy down coat completed the disguise. So far, other than a few fans who'd approached her at LAX, everyone had left her alone. Her Clark Kent, hide-in-plain-sight disguise either did its job or, more likely, it was Tucker—who glowered at anyone who came within four feet of her.

He had no disguise.

Which meant everyone had to know she was Kenzie.

So, yup. It was probably Tucker and his grumpy glowering that kept fans away.

There were also only a handful of people on the plane. Kenzie had a hunch Tucker had bought up the seats himself. Most of the other passengers had scattered when they landed, having only brought carry-on bags with them.

A Charlie Brown-style Christmas tree sat on the reservation desk nearby while "Run Run Rudolph" played over the airport speakers.

She and Tucker had found an easy rhythm with each other on the flight. Almost like friends. The other night they'd ordered Chinese food, and over steamed chicken and vegetables, she'd chilled and not chilled with him while they'd watched what felt like a bajillion episodes of *Arrested Development* before Leah had showed up to check on her and ruined it all.

Kenzie glanced to the main doors of the airport. No Tucker. After they landed, he took off to find out where his brother had left his truck in the parking lot. There was practically a blizzard going on outside, so he'd insisted she wait for their bags inside the warm luggage claim area.

She scribbled some dialogue into the notebook she always carried. Little snippets of ideas for her latest screenplay distraction always popped up at the strangest times.

Her phone pinged in her hand.

She glanced to the most recent message. Her mother was pissed. Kenzie was okay with that.

A little thrill of adrenaline at being disobedient pulsed through her.

*The party won't be the same without you. Please reconsider. Guests are attending to see *you*.*

She should really just block the number.

The chat bubbles pulsed, lord knew what her mother was typing. It didn't matter though. Kenzie was in Colorado because she had approximately one week to convince Tucker to do the damn song so she could salvage her career.

She typed out a response to whatever nonsense her mother was about to spew.

Having a great time with Tucker! Have fun at your party. No cell service at the ranch. Call Leah if you need anything. She knows how to reach me.

Kenzie stared at the screen. To send or not to send? The message would make her mother pop an aneurysm. She absolutely loathed Leah. Mostly because she'd taken her place as

Kenzie's manager. Also, because Leah didn't take her shit. Even more than that, her mother couldn't stand being out of touch with her daughter. They had a messed-up relationship, sure, and her mother thrived on Kenzie's fame. She didn't quite know how to show she loved her daughter, so hovering was her method of choice.

Kenzie's phone dinged.

This is such a disappointing way to end the year.

You're such a disappointment, Kenzie. That was what her mother meant.

Kenzie froze, her gaze fixed on the screen, her finger poised over the send button on the message she'd prepared. She did better when she took a break from her parents. Her mother was…well, her mother. And her father was…well, her father. He was the guy who'd left when she was a baby and then showed up after her first movie debuted when she was twelve, ready to reinsert himself into her life.

Leah handled his communication. Usually, he called when he was late with his mortgage payment or her half-siblings needed braces.

Her phone pinged.

I didn't raise you to take off when things get hard.

There it was. You're just like your father, Kenzie.

I'm saving my career. That was what she wanted to type. But she didn't.

She was waiting for the perfect time to approach Tucker about the song again. Once she found out what made him tick, what would convince him to do this for her, she'd work her magic.

Everyone had a button to push—a way to get them to do what they didn't want to do. The key was figuring it out and convincing them without letting on to what you were doing.

Some might call that manipulation. Kenzie chose to call it a mutually beneficial arrangement. Everyone walked away happy.

Her phone pinged again.

Electing not to respond to me is juvenile. I raised you better than this.

A light sweat formed along her hairline, and not because the heater in the airport was on and she wore a thick coat. No, there was only so much passive-aggressive nitpicking a girl could take. But she only had one mother. And Moira had done her best to get Kenzie where she was in life. Her warped idea of success as a parent meant her daughter was a household name.

She reread her unsent message.

Having a great time with Tucker! Have fun at your party. No cell service at the ranch. Call Leah if you need anything. She knows how to reach me.

She needed a break. Her mother could go through Leah. Kenzie pressed send on the aneurysm-inducing message.

Deep breaths. She turned off her phone and shoved it into the pocket of her coat.

"Your mom again?" Tucker sat beside her and handed over a disposable cup of hot chocolate. He'd wrapped a flimsy paper napkin around the sides.

A thin coat of snow and ice stuck to his Carhartt sweatshirt.

"It's always my mom." She held the top of the cup to her nose. The aroma of chocolate tickled her senses. "Where'd you get this?"

"There's a cart with coffee and stuff over there." He jerked his chin toward a little trolley by the TSA office.

"I don't think they meant that for us."

He shrugged. "Shoulda put a sign on it then."

One hand on his cup, he stretched the other arm behind her.

The hot chocolate called her name. *Kenzie. Be bad, Kenzie. Do the things you're not supposed to do. You're on vacation, Kenzie.*

There was no way she could drink anything with both dairy and sugar. She'd puff up like…well, her coat.

Still, she could smell it. She stuck her nose over the rim, inhaling the decadent scent of powdered cocoa product and dry milk mixed with water.

Heaven.

Tucker took a swig out of his own cup, a dab of chocolate at the corner of his lips. He licked at it.

Her belly took a little dive. Her cheeks heated. And she experienced internal tingles totally inappropriate for baggage claim.

"You going to drink that or just have a love affair with it?" he asked, his arm still behind her head.

"What are you talking about?" She angled herself toward him.

"You moaned when you sniffed your drink," he pointed out.

He lied.

"I did not."

He chuckled. "You did."

Had she? Fine. Maybe she had.

She inhaled more. What the hell. Rebel Kenzie was on vacation with a rock star. She could drink what she wanted. As a matter of fact, she should make some rules for her time with Tucker. Cell phone off. She could eat what she wanted. The only rule she'd have this trip? There were no rules.

A smile played on her lips as she wrapped them around the cup. A trickle of heated chocolate slid over her tongue… Holy shit. This stuff was amazing. When was the last time she'd had hot cocoa?

Nineteen ninety-five. Right before she'd become a child actress on that cable channel.

She took another sip.

Sometimes her nutritionist would slip her 80 percent dark chocolate as a treat. This was not that. That was bitter. This was…she took another sip.

When she got back home she was going to buy stock in a

hot chocolate company. Then it wouldn't matter if she didn't get any more movie parts because she could sit around in the California sun and drink hot cocoa.

Tucker cleared his throat.

She glanced to him.

"Seriously, Kenzie. You're practically making love to that cup."

"It's been a while." She shrugged and dabbed at her lips with the coarse napkin.

A flare of heat stirred in his eyes.

She rolled her eyes. "I mean since I've had hot chocolate, Tucker."

A slow smile spread across his cheeks. "What else have you been abstaining from?"

"Bread," she said, immediately. "Also, cheese. And sausage. Mind out of the gutter."

He paused, a strange intense look passing over his face.

Did she have cocoa on her lip or something? Absently, she wiped at her lips with the back of her hand. "What?"

His expression turned serious. "I want to kiss you."

"You've kissed me, Tucker."

A few times.

He leaned closer, so they shared the same air. "I want to see if it's always peach lip gloss."

Oh. Well. Hello. She was not expecting that.

But she was on vacation, and if this was a real do-what-she-wanted type event, she'd kiss Tucker. Not here, in the airport. They could kiss here, but that would hardly count. They needed a private kiss. Somewhere without her peach lip gloss.

She leaned into him, her lips brushing against his ear. "That's the lip stuff my makeup artist uses. When I do my own makeup it's just normal lip gloss."

The scent of Tucker—soap and male skin and leather—

along with the taste of chocolate created the Tucker-wants-to-kiss-me-*squee* buzz going on in her head.

"The peach flavor can be distracting," she continued, making her voice intentionally husky.

She moved back so their gazes met.

He quirked an eyebrow. "Is that right?"

"What I mean is, when I'm not at an event, it's just me. I'm just me." Just disappointingly me.

Something that looked a whole lot like desire sparked in his eyes. He was really close. She should just kiss him. It'd be fun. And that was what this was about. Fun. Also, getting her career back. Why not have some fun in the process?

"Then what do you taste like, exactly?" He leaned back as though nothing had passed between them, his attention totally focused on his chocolate.

Well, she didn't taste like peach lip gloss, that was for sure.

A feeling she'd become accustomed to when she was around him settled in her stomach. The little hairs on her arms raised, telling her someone was watching them. A camera shutter was about to snap.

It didn't matter, they weren't doing anything they weren't supposed to do. As a matter of fact, a baggage claim kiss caught on camera was probably something Leah would commend her for.

Still though, that feeling.

Of all the drippings of fame she hated most, this was it.

His phone buzzed. He held it to his ear.

"Where the hell is my truck?" Tucker said into the phone.

He'd lost his truck? That wasn't good.

"You caved?" His expression held firm, the little line over his eyebrow ticking in time with his pulse. "I cannot believe you did this." He shoved his finger against the little red icon on the screen and used an inventive string of profanity.

"You okay?" Kenzie asked, cautious.

Tucker glanced up, looking past her, and his face fell. "Shit."

"What's the matter?" She turned, expecting to see a slew of paparazzi or—given Tucker's expression—a pack of rabid squirrels.

None of that. Instead, it was a woman in her mid-sixties shuffling toward them on a pair of crutches with her ankle in a huge, black soft-cast boot. A scruffy-looking guy in a flannel shirt—no coat—strode beside her, his arm against her elbow even though she stopped every few feet to shoo him aside. He wore a cowboy hat. A real one. And he wasn't even on a movie set.

"Brace yourself," Tucker said under his breath.

"For what?" Mackenzie turned her focus to him.

He caught her gaze, rubbed a hand over his face, and shook his head. "For my parents."

Kenzie turned back to them.

These people had given birth to Tucker? Mackenzie studied them closer, a slow smile spreading all through her. Not that she was surprised that these two particular people had created him. It was more that he had parents at all. Tucker was larger than life. A living legend.

Kenzie stood.

"Mom doesn't know about us," Tucker said quickly and quietly. "About our arrangement. Dad figured it out, but he won't say anything."

"Oh. Okay." It hadn't felt very much like an arrangement just then.

"Mom talks to the press. Her name is Lori," he continued. His words were coming at the speed of light but so quiet she could almost believe they weren't being said at all. "Watch what you say. She means well, but she answers their questions without thinking. Dad's safe. He doesn't talk to anyone. The rest of the family keeps their lips sealed, too."

"What's your dad's name?" Kenzie asked.

"Clint." Tucker stretched his fingers then curled them back to his palm.

"Tucker." Kenzie put her hand on his shoulder. "It's okay. They're people. I'm a person. I'm sure we'll get along fine."

"I thought there'd be more time to prepare you for this. A whole car ride." Was Tucker starting to sweat? A thin film of perspiration formed along his forehead. Kenzie had seen the man give a concert in a massive stadium. He never showed his nerves.

Nervous Tucker was a brand-new experience.

"Hello, Mrs. McKay." Kenzie waved to the couple coming toward them.

They stopped. Tucker's mom said something to his father. She was a hand talker. Talking with one's hands probably wasn't a good idea when balance was an issue, as illustrated when she lost her grip on one of the crutches. It smacked against the industrial-tile floor of the airport.

Frantic, his mother glanced to Kenzie then back to Tucker's father.

Kenzie started toward her.

Tucker grabbed her arm. "No. You'll draw attention."

His father bent to grab the fallen crutch. His mother swung around back toward the sliding doors of the exit. She turned wide, the end of her crutch walloping Tucker's father against the back of his head.

"Oh my God." Kenzie froze.

"Find a distraction for the lady with the cell phone. Mom'll be mortified if this makes TMZ." Tucker handed off his cocoa and abandoned Kenzie to help his parents. His father was sprawled on the floor while his mother tried to help.

Tucker broke into a run.

Shit.

Kenzie glanced around.

A little girl tugged her mother's arm and pointed toward Tucker.

There were times Kenzie could pinpoint the exact moment when a normal fan turned into a videographer for the highest Hollywood bidder. This was one of those moments. The mother paused only a split second before fumbling with her phone.

Kenzie needed a distraction.

She was about to be a distraction.

She glanced to the cocoa in her hands. Her bag was coming around the carousel. She balanced the cocoa on the arm of her chair and stepped toward the cell-phone-camera wielding brunette. She pulled off the baseball cap she'd worn on the plane, a curtain of red hair falling over her cheek.

"Are you from Colorado?" she asked the woman before she had a chance to do anything more than get her phone into her palm.

The woman stilled, her expression suggested she'd known exactly who Kenzie was the whole time.

She said nothing. The shock on her face said everything for her—she couldn't believe Kenzie was speaking to her.

"This is my first time here," Kenzie continued as though this were a normal two-way conversation.

Her bag moved closer.

"Are you…?" The woman asked. She was so not being subtle with her cell phone.

"Mackenzie Bennett. That's me." Kenzie stepped in front of the woman so she couldn't easily get a photo of Tucker's parents. "Would you like a photo?" She nodded to the phone in the woman's hand with the open camera app. "I love doing selfies."

She loathed doing selfies. But she'd take one for the team here. Team Tucker.

"Really?" the woman asked.

Kenzie nodded.

They got cheek-to-cheek comfortable. The woman raised the phone. Kenzie smiled huge. The shutter sound clicked on the app.

"Thank you so much!" The woman gushed, checking the photo.

Kenzie glanced at the screen. She looked fine. But fine didn't cut it in this business. She sighed inside. Given that she had little makeup on and her hair was not even remotely camera ready, she could bet large sums of money she'd just made *In Time*'s "Worst Dressed of the Week" column.

Wasn't Christmas fun?

Chapter Eight

Kenzie was "oohing and aahing" at the cell phone screen. She laughed and continued to block the direct line of sight to his parents. She wasn't enjoying it though. Kenzie was a great actress, but he'd noted the concern on her face when she'd watched his mother accidentally beat the crap out of his father with her crutches. Now she protected his mother from embarrassment.

Tucker may not have been 100 percent falling for Kenzie before the trip. Even when she'd climbed right under his skin and kissed him at her front door. Even when he'd tripped over his own heart at Taylor's party when Kenzie had been so vulnerable. Even when he'd read the words she was worried no one would like and had gotten a glimpse right into her soul.

Kenzie wasn't a Hollywood fake. She was real—every part of the glamour and every bit of the down-to-earth. They were different facets to the diamond that she was.

But Kenzie taking care of his family? Yeah, he was about to be all in. The realization hit him in the solar plexus.

This was bad. This was not light.

When she did things like this, it made him believe that

someone else in the crazy entertainment industry put others first sometimes. He got so fucking tired of having to watch his back all the time. No one ever did things like Kenzie had just done.

And she'd done it for his mother.

In front of his father.

His father, who was not a fool and would know exactly what had gone down.

Which meant, Kenzie would have both his parents tucked in her pocket. Along with an idiot cowboy who was the tiniest shove from tipping over the precipice of giving this pretty girl with sharp green eyes anything she ever asked.

"Let me get that." Tucker grabbed Kenzie's suitcase from the conveyer.

"We're taking selfies. You should get in on this." Her eyes sparkled at him, practically broadcasting what she'd done. She tugged off her coat and dropped it on the suitcase.

He couldn't help himself, he ran a hand over her arm. Damn, her sweater was soft. Like her.

Deep breaths, Tucker.

"Sorry, I didn't catch your name." Kenzie used animated gestures as she talked to the woman with the camera.

The woman paused an abnormally long time before she spoke. "Connie."

Poor Connie's mouth stayed open like, well, his mother's had done when she'd caught sight of his starlet. Didn't take much to understand why. Kenzie giving you her undivided attention was panic-inducing the first time. She had a way of looking at a person and making them feel like they were the only one in her world.

That kind of attention was addicting.

"Are you my daddy?" The little girl holding the woman's hand tugged at his arm. Her face held the hope of a child at Christmas.

He took a close look at Connie. No, he hadn't… "Uh. Ha. Negative."

He scratched an invisible itch behind his ear.

Kenzie gave him side-eye. The edges of her eyelids crinkling just the tiniest bit.

"I'm so sorry. Ever since she read that book about a bird who goes around asking who his mother is, she asks everyone that question." Connie knelt to the child. "Daddy's at his meeting. Like we talked about."

She mouthed an "I'm sorry" and hustled to grab a suitcase on the other side of the conveyor belt.

"Tuck?" His father's voice rumbled behind him. "You gonna introduce your mother or what?"

He'd go with the "or what" option if that were truly a choice. As it turned out, his parents had decided to meet him at baggage claim and drive him and Kenzie to his ranch themselves. His brother was about to get an unpleasant phone call about follow-through. He'd promised to personally deliver Tucker's truck. A two-hundred-dollar bottle of scotch had been negotiated in return for the delivery. Looked like Tucker and Kenzie had a night ahead of them with a bottle of expensive booze.

"Mom. Dad. This is Kenzie." He rested his hand at the center of Kenzie's back.

This was nice. The two of them. His parents.

He shook his head.

This was not real.

"Mr. and Mrs. McKay." Kenzie shook his father's hand and then, holy shit, she leaned forward and hugged his mother. "It's lovely to meet you."

His mother stood unmoving.

Kenzie, unfazed by his mother's inability to form words continued, "Tucker's told me so much about you both."

That was lie number one. He'd told her literally nothing

about them—other than his mother wanting him to bring Kenzie home for Christmas.

"I mean, okay, so he hasn't actually told me that much. He's very protective of your family and likes to keep his personal life private. As someone with a mother who doesn't keep anything private—at all—I can appreciate his insistence on protecting all of you from the craziness of what we do for a living."

She paused. Smiling as though she was chatting with Jackson Hayes on the red carpet, giving sound bites, playing the part. Not chatting up his very small-town parents. "Tucker said my visit was a surprise for you. I take it someone spilled the tea?"

"Cord let it slip." Clint pursed his lips. "Ruined the whole thing."

Tucker would have words with his brother.

"I like your movies." Tucker's mother finally spoke to Kenzie. Her gaze flicked to Tucker, as if searching out how much she could safely say. "And I really like your teeth. They're so white. And your hair. It's very red."

Okay, well, he hadn't expected *that*.

Kenzie raised a hand to her red hair. "You are so sweet. Do you want to sit with me while Tucker gets the bag situation figured out? He didn't mention you'd hurt your foot."

His mother's face gentled. His father grinned like Santa the day after Christmas, when he had a whole year to chill before go-time again.

Yes, Tucker's family was falling for Kenzie, just like he was.

HOLY CRAP IT WAS FREEZING. Kenzie's California genes did not love the frigid Colorado blizzard temperatures.

She shivered in her down coat while Tucker guided her to

his parents' truck—one of those double-cab things with a set of two doors on each side—parked in the front row of the airport parking lot. Tucker wore no coat, just a sweatshirt. His father didn't have a coat on either, and his mother only wore a light jacket.

Meanwhile, Kenzie's teeth were clacking together even though she was inside a down parka.

His father had tossed the luggage in the bed of the truck and worked to cover it with a tarp. Tucker hopped up into the bed to help tie it down.

"Would you like to sit up front?" His mother led the way to the front passenger door.

Kenzie glanced to the woman's wrapped ankle. "No, you should sit there, Mrs. McKay. More room to stretch. I'll sit in the back with Tucker."

"Call me Lori. Mrs. McKay was my mother-in-law." Lori took a deep breath and stared a few beats too long at Kenzie.

She was used to it. Eventually, the novelty of what she did for work would wear off. It always did.

Tucker slid between the two of them and opened the front door for his mother. He gripped her arm to help her in, keeping the weight off of her ankle.

Kenzie climbed into the backseat. Tucker settled in beside her, and his father took the wheel.

"The family is excited to see you. They're all popping by in the morning to say hello," Lori chattered, her nerves showing.

Tucker frowned at his mother. "They're popping by because it's Christmas."

Lori reached over the seat to grab Kenzie's hand where it lay near the headrest. "Mostly because you're here though, dear."

Well, that wasn't frightening at all.

"We're stopping at the grocery on the way home. Do you

two need anything?" Lori released her hand and dug through her canvas over-the-shoulder purse.

Tucker frowned some more. "Cord said he'd stock the fridge. But I'm not trusting him to follow through on anything at this point."

"If he said he'll do it, he'll do it." His father replied.

Tucker's lips pressed together. "He said he'd drop my truck off, too."

They backed out of the spot, heading for the exit.

"Don't be mad. That's my fault. I insisted we pick you up." Lori turned in her seat and held out a package of Doublemint. "Gum?"

"Thanks." Kenzie slid a silver-wrapped stick of gum from the package. And a second for Tucker.

She handed it to him.

He unwrapped it, shoved it in his mouth, and crumpled the foil.

"How many brothers do you have?" Kenzie asked, doing her best to draw him into the conversation.

"Two brothers and three sisters. You can ignore all of them." He focused on the snow falling outside the window.

The slush under their wheels crunched as they drove slowly around a roundabout.

"Why would I ignore them?" She'd never had brothers and sisters. If she had, she would've loved them. Played with them. Spent all her time with them.

All she'd had were a bunch of producers and directors telling her what to do and where to stand.

"Best ignore the boys. A pretty girl shows up, those idiots go to automatic stupid." His father replied for Tucker.

Tucker nodded. "It's the truth."

Lori turned in her seat again, to face Kenzie. "They don't mean that. Our children are all very smart."

"I do mean that." Clint pulled to a stop at a red light. "Those boys can't keep their heads screwed on straight when anyone with a pretty smile and a set of boobs walks in the room."

Tucker dropped his head to his hands. "Dad. Really?"

Kenzie's focus pinged between them. Why try to get a word in when the show was so damn fun to watch?

"I think you'll find that the McKay kids all turned out great. Good stock. Healthy. The gene pool is really quite good. I'm probably biased, but Tucker will be a great father. Genetically, it's practically guaranteed." Lori winked at her.

"Mom, I'm not a stud bull. You don't need to pimp me out to Kenzie."

His father hit the gas, the wheels spinning in the snow, setting them back against the cloth seats. Kenzie gripped the seat belt crossing her chest.

"Can't see where it'd hurt." Clint glanced back to them in the rearview mirror. "You've been so busy dancing around on those stages. It's time to stick around at the ranch. Time to settle."

"I think he means settle down," Lori corrected, with a gentle hand to Clint's shoulder.

"What else would I mean?" He glowered at her, but he did it in such a way that Kenzie knew if Lori asked him for anything, he'd do it.

"Well, it kind of sounded like you meant that he's settling for Kenzie. But she's not the kind a man settles for." His mother turned in her seat. "Isn't that right, dear?" She turned back to her husband. "She's the real deal. He wouldn't be settling at all."

Clint huffed, his palm shifting them into second. "I never said he would be."

"No, you just implied it with the way you worded your sentence."

Kenzie's gaze shifted to Tucker.

Eyes closed, his head had dropped against the window

beside his head. He pinched the bridge of his nose and took a deep breath.

Kenzie could relate. She generally felt that way around her own mother.

PERHAPS HOLLYWOOD WASN'T SO bad, after all. Tucker shifted, and his hand skimmed the side of Kenzie's palm where it rested under her jacket. She pressed her hand closer to his. Gaze breaking away from the window, he caught the spark in her eyes and traced a fingertip in slow circles over her knuckles. A smile tickled the edge of her lips.

His parents were still yapping in the front seat, but right then he tuned them out. Focused on Kenzie.

Every nerve in his body was on alert. If she could do that to him with just a touch, he was done for if they ever managed to get naked together. She turned her hand palm-up and settled her fingers between his.

Contentment. That's what this was. The same feeling he had when the notes flowed on a new song. God, it'd been forever since he'd felt content.

Mom pointed to a glowing Safeway sign. "Turn here, hon."

"I'll turn at the other entrance." His dad jerked his chin ahead in illustration.

"No, that one spits you at the wrong side of the store. Do this one so you don't have to go over those speed bumps."

Parents distracted by parking lot decisions, Tucker leaned over so his lips met Kenzie's ear and only she could hear. "Sleeping arrangements? My parents have a guest room for you at their place. I have a guest room for you at the ranch. Or there is plenty of room in my bed. Your choice."

The skin of her cheek brushed his lips when she turned to whisper in his ear. "Not your parents' place."

His stomach dropped. In a good way.

Not his parents' place. He could live with that.

They pulled to stop, and his mother reached for the door handle.

His father laid a hand on her arm. "Stay put, it's icy."

He was using his I'm-being-reasonable-so-please-cooperate tone.

Mom shook her head. "You'll buy the wrong kind of ice cream."

His face was weathered, wrinkled, from years of working outside. But when he looked at Tucker's mother, the lines smoothed. Even if his words were gruff, his expression mellowed. "It's the one with that rabbit on the side. I'll remember."

"No, we need spinach and avocados, too. I'm coming." His mom turned to Kenzie. "I've been making celebrity diet shakes. Have you tried them?"

Heaving a breath, his father left the cab of the truck, circling around the hood to Tucker's mother's door.

"With ice cream?" Kenzie's eyebrows puckered together.

"That wasn't in the original recipe, but that one didn't taste good at all. Add a little ice cream and it does just the trick." Mom pushed open the door and scooted from the truck. His father handed over her crutches and pushed the door closed.

"Ice cream makes everything better." Tucker squeezed Kenzie's hand.

His parents disappeared through the sliding doors of the grocery store, past the inflatable Santa and the Salvation Army guy with the collection bucket ringing his bell.

Kenzie squeezed his fingers back. "I'll have to try one of your mom's shakes."

"Kale, avocado, spinach, and ice cream. Yum," Tucker said with fake enthusiasm.

Kenzie grabbed the notebook she kept with her, scribbling something on the pages.

"What're you working on?"

"Nothing." Absently, she jotted more notes in chicken scratch he couldn't make out.

"Doesn't look like nothing."

"Another screenplay. Sometimes little ideas come to me, hence the—" She held up the notebook.

"That's fantastic." He missed doing that, finding fragments of ideas and letting them out on a sheet of paper. Letting the rhythm of the words do their thing.

"Do you ever miss this part? The creating?"

Only all the time. "Yeah."

She paused. Thoughtful. "Then you should write that song for Eileen."

No way in hell. Even if his muse hadn't deserted him. "Eileen's impossible."

Kenzie shrugged. "Still, it'd be awesome if you did it."

"Why are you so interested in this?" He shifted to turn to her, his seat belt cutting across his shoulder.

"No reason." Her hair hid her expression so he couldn't read her.

"Kenzie."

She released a drawn-out breath. "I'm up for the lead in Eileen's movie. I want it to be successful. And you doing the song would kind of be an endorsement after the whole toaster thing."

Tucker's gut tipped. He should've corrected that right away. "Even if I wanted to work with Eileen, which I don't, I haven't been able to write anything in over a year."

Might as well let Kenzie in on his dirty secret.

Her green eyes got huge. "Seriously?"

He nodded. "Hence the whole band blowing up and retirement thing."

"Tucker, I'm so sorry." Her palm rested against his biceps.

Her touch felt nice. Good. Right.

He reached for her, the skin of her jaw soft under the pads of his fingertips. He traced the soft spot to her neck. Her mouth parted.

Seat belt unhooked, he scooted across the bench seat into her space.

Lifting a handful of red hair, he breathed in the scent of vanilla and flowers. Her signature scent. She'd bottled it. Sold it. But it didn't smell like this on anyone else. Not that he'd gone around sniffing women, but he'd smelled it in a bottle.

On Kenzie the scent was everything. She was her own brand of intoxication.

"Are you going to kiss me? Or what?" Her lips grazed the air above his cheek, the little hairs there standing at attention.

His mouth met hers, subtle then hungry.

"Oh my lord. Clint, they're kissing." His mother's voice pierced the moment. "Just like in that movie she did with Carter Pearson."

Tucker jerked back. Kenzie cleared her throat.

And the moment was gone.

Thanks to his mother's love of movies and Carter Pearson.

Chapter Nine

They were holding hands. A silent link that looped them together during the ride to his ranch while his parents chattered away in the front seat. Kenzie gave the right answers on cue, but her mind stayed in the backseat. Focused on Tucker.

Every time he stroked the fleshy part above her thumb, she got goosebumps like she was a teenager. Yes, Kenzie had butterflies in her stomach. A whole swirling mass of them.

"Kenzie, do you have any special requests for Christmas breakfast tomorrow?" Lori's neck was going to have a kink in it from the amount of time she spent turned around. Though, she didn't seem to mind.

They turned off the highway onto a two-lane winding road leading them through a canyon onto what Tucker called the Grand Mesa. A massive flat-topped mountain with his town of Collbran somewhere near the top.

The snow had stopped, leaving a film of white powder on the trees, the road, the outside of the truck.

"Anything will be great," Kenzie replied. "I can help, too."

She loved to bake but rarely got the chance.

"Everybody brings something. We do it potluck style," Lori said.

Kenzie hadn't been to an event where they did "potluck style" since she was five. How fun was this?

"What were you planning to bring?" Kenzie asked Tucker, her enthusiasm lacing her words.

The little crinkles around his eyes bunched. "Whatever's in the pantry."

Clint harrumphed.

He had the act of being the gruff patriarch down to an art, but his eyes told a whole different story. They were among the kindest eyes Kenzie had ever seen. Honest eyes. The kind of eyes that told a story. Clint would've made an excellent actor. Ninety percent of getting an audience to believe the story was having eyes that sparkled with truth—even when you played a role. "Last year he brought a jar of mayonnaise."

"And we used that mayonnaise on sandwiches at lunch." Lori flashed Tucker an it's-okay-sweetie smile.

Kenzie glanced to Tucker's profile. "Did your brother leave flour, butter, all that?"

"If not, come by early tomorrow. I have it all," Lori assured.

Baking with Tucker's family sounded…really nice. Fun, even.

"That would be great." Kenzie settled back into her seat, content.

"What are you planning on making?" Tucker squeezed her hand.

She shrugged. "Whatever I can find a recipe for."

The two-lane road led through the canyon, a frozen creek along one side. Tucker leaned over her and pointed out the window. "Keep your eye out for deer."

Kenzie squinted in the direction he'd pointed. "Like, wild deer?"

Tucker's lips played into a smile. "You'll see them along the edge of the road sometimes. There was one just there. Watch. There are usually several grouped together."

"They'll bounce right in front of the truck. They're pretty, but they're stupid," Clint went on. "Not like mountain lions. Those are smart. Fast. They'll pounce on you before you have a moment to process what's happening."

"Wait, there are mountain lions?" Kenzie shot Tucker a look.

The jerk was laughing. "Yeah. There are some around here."

"Like, there are mountain lions at your ranch?" Kenzie asked. Just to confirm.

She glanced outside again, leaning close against the window. Her breath fogged the glass.

"Mountain lions eat the deer," Lori said, as though it was the most normal thing in the world.

"You said nothing about wild animals when we talked about this," Kenzie hissed to Tucker.

"There're bears, too." Clint went on.

"Not alongside the road though," Lori reassured.

"Oh my God." What kind of hell had Tucker brought her to? She preferred human monsters over animal monsters.

"Don't worry about the bears, dear. Just make lots of racket if you see one. Avoid the cubs. They're cuter than the dickens, but their mamas get real mean about things." Lori waved a hand. "You'll be fine."

"Tucker, you didn't say there were wild animals," Kenzie whispered again with more force.

"They don't come up to the houses much. You'll be fine," he repeated his mother's words, squeezing her now-cold hand.

Kenzie wouldn't be leaving the house, apparently.

Her mind filled with gory details of what mama bears did to actresses who got too close to their babies.

"Kenzie?" Tucker asked.

"Hmm?"

"It's winter. The bears are all asleep for a few months."

"What about the mountain lions?"

"They're awake," Clint interjected.

"How far is Vail from here?" Maybe the vultures at her mother's party weren't so bad, after all?

"A few hours east, if the weather is good," Clint replied.

"You're not leaving, are you?" Lori turned, her expression concerned. "Tucker won't let anything happen to you. You can't leave now. It's almost Christmas. We need to bake together."

Kenzie's heart spasmed. Lori really wanted her there, and not because she wanted Kenzie to do anything for her. Kenzie could get used to that.

"I guess I'll just stay inside."

Tucker ran a hand over her hair, tucking it behind her ear. "That can be fun, too."

Their gazes met, he winked, and her hands were miraculously warm again. As was the rest of her body.

"Yup. Sure can." Lori started talking with her hands again. "We set up board games by the fireplace, football on the television. The kids on Christmas morning make it all worth it. It's so much fun."

Kenzie glanced to Tucker. His lips flattened into a smile. He bit at his knuckles in an apparent attempt to stop laughing.

"It sounds nice." Kenzie whacked the side of his thigh where it lay under her coat.

Tucker snatched her hand and made a slow move of lacing his fingers with hers. Her pulse thrummed. His thumb traced figure eights on the top of her hand, setting every nerve in her body on alert.

She had a feeling board games had nothing on inside games with Tucker.

WELL, his parents had thoroughly wigged out Kenzie.

They turned the corner to his driveway. Darkness had settled over the mountain, the moon making the crystals in the snow shimmer. The truck passed under the Bandit Ranch sign that hung across the entry to his property—a large log on each side of the drive and one across the top with the sign on hinges, marked his official return home.

He felt…

He felt no different.

Dammit. He'd hoped maybe when he passed over the threshold to his land something would click. A feeling of things being right.

Nope. The only thing that felt right was Kenzie's hand in his. They'd practically been intimate on the drive—with only their fingers stroking each other.

His parents had no idea what was going on under that coat between them.

They pulled up to the main house. His house.

Cord had the lights inside blazing to welcome him. At least the asshole could follow through with something.

He opened the door at the same time his father climbed out of the truck. Kenzie gave his mother an awkward over-the-seat hug and scooted out after him.

She blasted past Tucker to the front door. Arms crossed, she fidgeted a little dance from foot to foot.

Yeah, his parents had freaked her out. He'd never seen anyone move so fast up the four front steps to his wrap-around pine deck.

He used his key and pushed the front door open. He'd picked it himself. Curved across the top, it had two sides that opened and heavy black metal hinges. "No mountain lions up here on the porch."

She rushed inside. "You can't know that."

He bit back a laugh.

A trip for the bags and he stood at the front of his house with his father.

"Son." Dad put out his hand.

Tucker shook it.

"Thanks, Dad."

"I like her." Dad had a firm grip.

"Me too." Acknowledging that made him warm all over.

A quick pump of the hand and his dad strode back to his truck. He stopped. Turned. "Don't fuck it up."

Well, there he had it.

With that, Tucker went inside to Kenzie.

"This house…" Kenzie turned a full circle in his living room.

His sister had decorated the place, he couldn't take the credit there, but he loved every bit of it. From the twenty-foot ceiling and the bank of windows along the south wall, to the stone fireplace and walnut hardwood floors. On one side there was a kitchen and dining room. The other had four bedrooms and a special recording studio he'd added before his muse had left him.

His sister was also likely responsible for the Christmas tree next to the fireplace. It nearly reached the ceiling.

Kenzie faced him. "Thank you for bringing me here."

She was too damn far away. Their bags abandoned by the front door, he moved to her.

Neither of them said a word. But in that nothing, they said everything.

Her red hair spilled over her shoulders. Lifting a curl, he wound it around his finger, released it and ran a hand over her shoulder. She took a sharp breath at the touch. He trailed his fingers down her arm to her hand, linking it with his.

She lifted onto her toes, pressing her lips to his.

The slow burn they'd started in the car lit to a full flame.

He tilted his head, the kiss turning to tongue and hands and their bodies molding together.

"Hey, Tucker," his sister's voice murdered the moment.

Kenzie pulled away, covering her mouth with the edge of her thumb.

"Oh my gosh." Sierra stepped backwards down the hallway she'd come from. "I had no idea. I'm sorry. I just brought…dinner."

She lifted the casserole dish as if it held the explanation for everything in life.

Chapter Ten

"What're you two doing?" Tucker asked.

Kenzie and Sierra were in his kitchen, scrolling through something on Sierra's phone.

"Figuring out what I'm bringing to Christmas breakfast tomorrow." Kenzie pointed to something on the screen. "Do we have any jam?"

"I don't know. Mom makes some blackberry preserves in the summer. She probably left some here. This one could work." Sierra rummaged through a cupboard next to the stove. "Yes! I knew Mom wouldn't let us down."

Kenzie gave her a high five.

They'd all eaten dinner together. He couldn't exactly kick his sister out when she'd provided the meal. He'd gone to check the barn and had only been gone fifteen minutes. Apparently, his sister and Kenzie had become good friends in that time. Which was nice. Except it was time for Sierra to leave. He needed to have Kenzie all to himself again.

"Check this out, Tucker." Kenzie motioned for him to join their huddle. "It's an app thing. You put in the ingredients you have and it tells you what you can make. Then it gives you the recipe."

He lifted a shoulder. "Don't need a recipe for a jar of mayo."

"We're making a blackberry French toast bake." Kenzie transferred the recipe to her notepad

She glanced up, beamed at him, and his heart spasmed against his ribcage.

Fuck it all. He was going to make blackberry French toast. And he was probably going to enjoy it.

"Do you want me to stay and help?" Sierra asked, all sincere like she wasn't barging into their evening.

"I think we got it." Tucker assured her, using any telepathic abilities he might possess to encourage her to skedaddle.

Sierra glanced between him and Kenzie. "Well, then it's time for me to leave. Kenzie, Merry Christmas."

"Goodnight." Kenzie gave his sister a hug.

Kenzie fitting in with his family should have concerned him. It should have made him want to pack her up and ship her back to California. It should have made him break out in hives.

It did none of that.

Sierra patted his arm on the way by. "See you in the morning, Tucker. Don't mess up the French toast."

"Okay." He rubbed his hands together. "What do we do?"

Kenzie directed the show. He cut the bread into chunks. She melted the preserves over the stove. He found a brick of cream cheese and cut it into slices. She mixed together eggs and milk and God knew what else.

He slid the pan onto a shelf in the refrigerator to set overnight.

Wiping his hands on a kitchen towel, he watched Kenzie as she scribbled more words in her notebook. Given the way her eyebrows bunched together and her lips puckered, she wasn't transcribing a recipe. He knew that look. The look of an artist with a story to tell.

A niggle of jealousy scratched because the words came to her and not to him. Even so, she felt right, here in his home. Usually having people in his space set his teeth on edge. But Kenzie? No, she fit.

He ran a hand up the side of her arm. She leaned into his palm and dropped her head against his chest, giving him her weight.

Gladly, he held her up.

The snow fell outside the window, snuggling the house in the muffled softness. Just like Kenzie did for him.

"Your family is really awesome."

"I don't want to talk about my family." He let his breath play against the sensitive skin of her earlobe. "And you didn't answer me in the car. Where should I put your bags?"

She relaxed further against him. "What are we doing?"

He found the hem of her sweater and let his fingertips trace the top of her jeans, around the side of her hip to her navel. "I think we're having a vacation."

She turned to him, wrapping her arms around his neck. "I don't have sex with men just because they want me to."

Immediately, he pulled back. "Kenzie"—he held his hands up in surrender—"I thought you wanted this, too. I didn't mean…" He took another step back, giving her space. "I thought you were into this—"

Confusion laced her expression. "I am."

"Then what's with the declaration?"

She crossed her arms over her chest. "I like you, Tucker."

"Okay."

"And I think you're one of the best men I've ever met."

"Why do I feel a 'but' coming on?"

"No, that's not it. I want to make it clear that I don't just sleep with the guys Leah pairs me with. This is different. You're different."

"Because you like me." It wasn't a question.

"Well, yeah. I don't usually like people. I mean, they're fine. In general. I guess I'm saying, I feel safe with you."

Better song lyrics he couldn't have written. For the first time in months, his fingers itched for a pen. To write down what she'd said. Put it to music.

His heart beat loudly beneath his ribs. He took a step forward. "There are a lot of assholes in the world."

"No kidding." She flicked her hair over her shoulder.

"I'm not one of them. I don't know exactly what's brewing between us here, but it feels right. For the first time in a long time, it feels right," he heard himself say the words, but his mind was in a separate place. The place he went when he was drafting a song. He hadn't been there in forever. Where the hell was that pen? His guitar? Fuck, a keyboard would even work right now, and he was shit when it came to piano work.

Absently, his fingers echoed the beat of his heart as they tapped the rhythm of the song against his thigh. It pulsed through him, around him, seeming to fill the room even though he knew, logically, it was only in his head.

His muse had picked a pretty crappy time to show up.

Kenzie was ready for him, and all he could think about was writing down song lyrics and putting them to music.

Palms against his chest, she stepped into him, lifted up onto her toes and pressed her lips against his. He wrapped his arms around her waist, his hands finding the hem of her sweater again, lifting it to touch the smooth skin underneath.

Mouth open, Kenzie kissed him like he was everything. Right then, it felt like pretty damn much everything. Their lips moved against each other. Her hands gripped the material of his sweatshirt, while his ran up her back to the clasp of her bra.

"Your bed," she said against his mouth, barely breaking the kiss to say the words before diving right back in.

Somehow, he managed to both lead the way to his

bedroom and still keep his lips on hers. This was a talent he'd never known he possessed. Given the moans she made against his mouth, she was totally on board with the progression of events.

The door of his bedroom stood ajar. He kicked it further open with his heel.

Both of them breathing heavily, they separated, their gazes locking even as he pulled off his socks and boots and she undid the clasp on her jeans so they slipped to the floor. Arms crossed in front of her, she lifted the sweater over her head in one motion. Her pale-pink bra matched the discarded sweater and the edge of lace on her panties.

Sonofabitch, Kenzie was in his bedroom in nothing but her lingerie, and he was damn well going to take a second to enjoy it.

Turned out that was all he got because it took only that long for her to go to work on his belt buckle.

Mackenzie Bennett was a wildcat in the bedroom.

Who. Knew.

He dropped his hands, letting her do whatever the hell she wanted with his body. She lifted his sweatshirt and kissed along the middle ridge of his abs. Her hands found their way between his legs, and she ran them along the hard length of him under the denim. He itched to touch her, but this was her show right now. And he was all about letting artists do their work. So, he refrained.

Licking her way down his stomach, she yanked his belt through the loops in a fast motion that left his head spinning.

She practically purred as she pulled his jeans over his hips, humming to herself in between the licks and kisses.

There was no blood left in his brain because it had all traveled south.

He pulled his shirt off, kicked his jeans aside, and lifted her to the end of the bed. He hadn't given much thought to the bed when he bought it, but between the bedframe and the memory-foam-topped mattress, the thing was higher than the usual setup. As Kenzie scooted herself back to his pillows, he realized the height might come in handy for a few of the positions her presence inspired, and since she'd picked his bed and not the guest room, he had every intention of trying them all.

He didn't climb on after her. Instead, he turned and took five steps toward the dresser, dug around the back of the top drawer and found the box of condoms he'd stored there. He tore into the box, grabbed several—they'd need them—and turned on his heel.

He stopped cold.

In the time it'd taken him to grab supplies, she'd lost the lingerie.

He was a celebrity. He knew better than anyone that celebrities were just people with jobs that made everyone feel like they deserved a piece of their lives.

But for the first time, he was starstruck.

His mouth dropped open, he gripped the protection in his hand, and he couldn't find any words. So instead he just said, "Kenzie."

In response, she spread her thighs and ran her hand over herself, doing what he should be doing but putting on a damn good show for him. It was like the first time they saw one another and neither could look away. But this time she was touching herself and he was invited.

Lucky. Him.

It had taken him five steps to get to the dresser but it only took three to get back to the bed. Their gazes locked the entire time. He crawled to her and kissed the arch of her foot. He kissed up her ankle, over her right calf, stopping to suck at the sensitive skin behind her knee. He continued up her leg, gentle kisses, slow kisses, to where her fingers rubbed the sensitive nub between her thighs.

Condoms abandoned on the bedspread, he lifted her hand from herself.

"Tucker, I'm almost…"

He wrapped his mouth around her fingers, sucking deep. Mackenzie on his tongue, she stopped talking. A gargled sound came from her throat and she pressed her head into the pillows.

Still sucking her fingertips, he replaced them with his own hand, sliding a finger inside, then two, and using his palm where she'd been working herself.

Her body bucked against his hand.

He released the suction on her fingers and moved his mouth to her center. She was saying something he couldn't make out, but given her hands pressing his face right where he wanted it, between her thighs, he was sure she was on board with what he had planned with his tongue.

His erection hard against the bedspread, he made love to her with his mouth. She wrapped her legs around his shoulders. Kenzie didn't talk in bed, but she made a lot of noises. It was on a loud moan that she came on his tongue, her body tensing before relaxing.

He kissed her hip, licked at her navel, and wanted to hug whatever life choices had brought him to this moment. Grabbing a condom from the pile, he continued his trek up her body, pausing at her breasts to give them an abundant amount of attention.

His dick pressed hard against her core, ready for release. He made his way to her neck. Then her jaw. She purred at him.

He found her lips and kissed her, eyes open, connected.

He pulled back, raising himself up over her. "Hi."

She chuckled. "Well, hey there."

"Merry Christmas to me." He nuzzled his face against her neck, letting his erection tease her opening.

"Merry Christmas to both of us." She draped her arm

over her forehead, her breast against his pec, her nipple hard against his.

He lifted off of her. Tore open the condom. She sat up and plucked it from his hand, reaching for his shaft before he could do anything more. Hand covering him, she gave a small squeeze, and then Mackenzie Bennett dropped her mouth to him and sucked.

Yes, his life choices were pretty damn good.

Hands in her brilliant red hair, he pinched his eyes shut and rode the wave of her impressive mouth. She slid her tongue over the head of him and he nearly finished right there. Four times. Four times she filled her mouth with him and slid to the tip, then back to the root.

He was pretty sure he was making the same noises she'd made before.

A thin pressure slipped over the top of his erection. He opened his eyes as she rolled the condom down the length of him.

TUCKER MCKAY WAS BUILT like a tank, with a penis the size of her arm. Okay, that was an exaggeration. But the erection fairies had used all of their fairy dust on this man.

Kenzie finished rolling on the condom and watched as he gripped himself at the root. It had never been like this with a man before. All consuming. Every nerve wired and alive.

She lay back into her nest of pillows and spread her legs for him. He pushed up over the top of her.

That wasn't exactly where she wanted it to go.

Her whole body squirmed. "I want you, Tucker."

His hands grabbed both of hers and held them over her head. "Say it again."

"I want you." Gah, her voice sounded so rough. So unrefined.

She cleared her throat.

His erection pressed against her belly as he kissed the tip of her nose. Her arms still held over her head, his thumb stroked her palm.

"I like it," he announced.

"What?"

"All of you." He shifted and pressed the tip of himself at her entrance. She moaned and scooted as he started to fill her.

His grip on her wrists tightened. He smiled against her mouth. Filled her in one move.

She gasped, complete and sated.

Tucker's mouth had nothing on the rest of him.

She'd been to one of his concerts, and he didn't just own the stage, he owned the whole damn stadium. Used every inch of the stage. Made a stadium of fifty thousand screaming fans feel like an intimate concert. An intimate concert with confetti cannons, a fog machine, and laser lights. Still, though, he could make a huge venue seem small when he took the stage.

It was his eyes, the way they saw everything—saw her for her, not as the woman on the screen—that did her in.

And that was the moment she was pretty sure she fell in love with a rock 'n' roll cowboy.

Chapter Eleven
CHRISTMAS DAY

Morning light filtered through the floor-to-ceiling windows, spilling over Tucker as he bent over his guitar. Not an electric one, like he played on stage. This guitar was acoustic. Like one a cowboy would play. The cowboy he was.

The storm had started and stopped in the night, leaving another rich layer of snow outside. Kenzie snuggled deeper into the bed, embracing the comforter and the way the snow muffled even the inside sounds.

Except the ones Tucker made.

It was Christmas, and this was her favorite present of all. Time with Tucker, watching him work.

Kenzie didn't dare say anything to ruin the moment. She was naked and in Tucker's bed while he strummed a song she'd never heard before. Eyes shut, his head down, he hummed the melody while his fingertips had their way with the strings. He paused, wrote something on the pad of paper beside him, and went back to his guitar.

His hair brushed against his ears. His forehead was completely relaxed.

Tucker was in his zone.

Then he sang a few bars, faint and barely there. His voice

wasn't smooth. Not like the musicians who seemed to have taken over pop music. Tucker's sounded scarred, low and husky. That sound that had captured audiences and sold millions of records.

She could listen to him like this forever and never get tired of it.

"What's another word for different?" He lifted his head to her.

She jolted when his blue eyes met hers. The matter-of-fact way he asked the question implied he'd known she was totally awake for a while.

"Sorry. What?" she replied.

"I need another word for different."

She let the question settle into her brain. "Distinct?"

"Thanks." He nodded and scribbled on his notepad. Hummed a bit more. His fingers continued massaging the strings on the guitar. "What about little?"

Was she actually helping Tucker write a song? "Small?"

"Nah, that's not it. Like little and fragile." He set the guitar aside. Rubbed a hand over his face.

"Did you sleep?" She sat up, the comforter sliding to her waist.

She needed to find her luggage. Get dressed. Make French toast.

He stared at her, his nostrils flared. "No."

"You've been at this all night?" Legs tossed over the side of the bed, she stood.

"Mmm hmm. Spent some time in the studio, but the lyrics come easier here." He did look beat—the whites of his eyes were red from him being up all night.

Heading to the attached bathroom for a shower, she paused with her hand on the doorframe and turned back toward him.

"Delicate." The word popped out of her mouth before she realized why she said it.

"Hmmm?" He rose his eyebrows.

"The word you're looking for is 'delicate.' Like 'little' but breakable. That's 'delicate.'"

He grinned a lopsided smile. "You're good at this. You should write songs. Half the battle is figuring out different words that mean the same thing."

"I'm more of a screenplay girl. I wouldn't know where to start with lyrics."

"I've been thinking a lot about your screenplay. I read it. It's exceptional." He set his guitar aside, stood, and stretched. He'd tossed on a pair of jeans at some point, but his torso was uncovered. "And I think you should produce your story. Not someone else. You. You'll do it justice."

Wait. He liked it?

"You don't think it's just scribbles?" She'd officially completed two entire sets of scribbles that would each film into about a two-hour flick.

"It's never only scribbles, Kenz." He crossed to her and kissed her in the familiar way they now had after the night they'd spent together…before she'd fallen asleep. "And what you wrote is definitely not scribbles. You're good at it."

The heat of a blush crept up her neck at the compliment. She leaned into him, ready to change the subject. "How'd you know I was awake? Before."

His hand slid to her naked bottom, scooting her into the bathroom, right against the counter. "You'd been staring at me for twenty minutes."

She smiled against his mouth, planting a kiss at the edge. "You never even looked up."

"Some things a guy just knows." His hands began roaming across her body like she was a new instrument he was ready to play.

Her skin heated. He gripped her backside and set her on the counter.

Arms around his neck, she poured herself into the kiss.

The fly of his jeans pressed against her already-wet core. She reached for the button between them, flicking it open and sliding her hand into his boxers.

His head fell back when she gripped him, but his hands stayed at her hips. Pressed there.

Then someone knocked on the bedroom door. More like, someone pounded on the bedroom door.

"Hey, asshole," a male voice said against the wood. "Rise and shine, it's Christmas."

"I'm going to kill my brother," Tucker said, the heat of the mood dissipated.

She released him. "Why is he here?"

"Who the hell knows? He's family. They come and go whenever they want. I think I need new locks on the doors." He put himself back together, buttoning his pants.

The counter was suddenly chilly against her bottom. He helped her down, setting her gently so her feet planted on the cushy bath rug, but his hands lingered on her waist.

She ran a palm over his abs, around his back, holding him against her. "I'm going to shower."

"I'll grab your bags." He said the words, but he made no move to leave. Instead, he laid light kisses along her shoulder, over the curve of her neck.

"Then we'll head to your parents'. Don't let me forget the French toast."

"And a jar of mayo." He leaned away and did the lopsided grin thing, making the dimple under his eye pop.

A quick press of his lips against hers, and he left. Closing the bathroom door behind him. Leaving her totally exposed. And not because she wasn't wearing any clothes.

Chapter Twelve

Kenzie fit right in.

After the ride to the ranch with his parents, he hadn't questioned how Kenzie slipped so easily into his family dynamic, but seeing the reality with everyone together was something amazing.

Something that made his heart feel complete.

His five-year-old nephew had taken up residence on Kenzie's lap while she read him some story about a mouse at Christmas.

His parents had a normal-sized tree filled with all the Christmas ornaments he and his siblings had made over the years in school. At the top, his mother had used a cowboy hat instead of a star. The house was warm—and not just in temperature. It was the kind of house you could take a nap in. Lay down on the sofa and fall asleep. When you woke up? Someone would've tucked a blanket over you. One his mother had knitted herself.

Kenzie ate it up.

His family ate her up.

Cord and Brody obviously acted like idiots, but he could tell they were happy. Tucker had finally found *his* happy.

Sierra, Jenny, and Cassidy? They were on cloud nine with Kenzie in the kitchen helping dish up food, Kenzie in the living room telling jokes, Kenzie on the sofa cuddling Jenny's kids.

His nephew scrambled off of Kenzie's lap to head for pancakes in the kitchen. Kenzie opened the bag she'd brought along and took out a little blue box. She handed it to his mother. "I didn't know what you'd like. So, I figured I'd get you something I'd like."

His mother was going to have a stroke. Right there.

"Merry Christmas," Kenzie continued.

Mom fussed over the box, the white ribbon, the little card Kenzie had attached before they'd headed over. Inside the box was a blue pouch. Inside the blue pouch was a diamond tennis bracelet.

Tucker grinned. His mother started to cry. "Oh my. Oh my."

Her fingertips tripped over the latch, trying to get the bracelet around her wrist. Kenzie stepped in and helped her.

For his father? She handed him a bottle of rum. "I picked it up on one of the sets when we were filming a pirate movie a few years ago. I hope you like it."

"Well…" His father looked over the bottle and stood. Cleared his throat. Ambled to the kitchen.

Kenzie looked to Tucker, her expression panicked.

Tucker reached for her hand. "That means he likes it. He's getting cups."

Sure enough, his dad returned with a stack of clear plastic cups. They didn't do dishes on Christmas morning. Instead everything was served on paper and in plastic.

Dad handed Tucker a cup of rum, and he took a slug. Good stuff.

Kenzie got a cup too, and she took a big drink.

Something about that made the whole thing even more real. Kenzie had told him at the beginning that she didn't drink in public because she couldn't relax when she was "on." The fact that she'd taken a sip around his family, meaning she was relaxed enough to do it, meant everything.

"Tucker?" She unlinked their hands and dug through her bag, handing him a box only slightly bigger than his mother's.

He tore off the paper. Inside was a photo of her in a small silver frame. Behind her, in the photo, was him.

This had been snapped at one of his concerts.

"That's when I saw you in Central Park, before we ever knew each other." She pointed to him in the background of the image.

He remembered that concert. Things had been going so well for him then. He'd been on top of the world.

And she'd been there.

In his father's words, "Well…" he heard himself say.

Tucker cleared his throat.

"That means he likes it," Sierra chimed in.

"I do." Tucker stood and grabbed a box from under the tree. The one Jessica had marked to Kenzie from him. He had no idea what she'd bought. He'd asked her to grab something and ship it ahead of time. At the time, it had made sense. In the now, it seemed like a really stupid idea.

Kenzie took her time with the paper. Glancing up at him in intervals, her eyes misting. She pulled a pink silk scarf from the tissue.

She stilled, a frown on her beautiful mouth. Quickly, she rearranged her expression into one of happiness. But he'd caught it. He'd messed up. It was clear as hell he hadn't bought it for her. He would never have shopped for a lacy scarf.

"It's really pretty. Thank you, Tucker." She moved in and kissed his cheek.

His mother's cell phone buzzed on the coffee table. "Everyone I know is here," she said, glancing to the screen. "Hello?"

"He's here…yes…hold on." She handed him the phone. "It's your manager."

Tucker snagged the cell. "Merry Christmas," he said into the microphone.

"Are you with Mackenzie?" Jessica asked, all business, no holiday.

"Yeah." Tucker glanced to her.

"I've been trying to reach you since yesterday," Jessica continued.

It's not like Tucker had any reason to be in contact with his manager over Christmas.

"My cell's been off. It's Christmas. I'm enjoying the family," Tucker responded. Though, truthfully, he'd mostly enjoyed Kenzie.

"Go someplace she can't hear," Jessica directed, like this was a CIA spy call.

Tucker's stomach pitched, and not in a good way. What the hell was going on?

"Sure." Tucker stood and headed for the kitchen. "What's up?"

"Mackenzie told Eileen you'd do a song for a movie. Signed a contract with the studio that says once you agree, she gets lead credit."

That was what she was getting at in the truck. And back at the premier. None of this was real. This was Kenzie using him to get her way. To advance her career.

"That doesn't sound right. I think you're mistaken." Although, in all the time he and Jessica had worked together, Jessica had never been mistaken.

"She didn't mention doing a song for a movie?"

Well, yeah, she had.

"I don't think it's like that." God, he hoped it wasn't like that.

He walked to the doorway and glanced to Kenzie. She looked up, her expression concerned.

He did his best to appear relaxed. Even crossed his ankles and leaned against the doorjamb.

"Got a copy of the contract right here. Says she's got until the new year to get you on board. Rumor has it, she went to Colorado to get under your skin. Make this happen."

"Who sent it to you?" Tucker asked.

"I've got people watching all corners of the industry. It's my job."

"You're sure?" Of course she was sure. This was Jessica.

"I'm sure."

"Thanks for the heads-up." Tucker turned off his phone. Stared at Kenzie while she laughed at something his sister Cassidy was saying.

The room went from warm and happy to a slow-motion massacre. The massacre being to his heart.

Kenzie glanced to him again. Her eyebrows puckered. "Tucker?"

She'd probably said his name, that's what it looked like she'd said. But there was no sound in the room right then. Not for him. Not when his world was flipping upside down.

"Kenzie." He was going to ask her. Right here. This involved his family, too. They deserved to know if she'd done this. "Jessica said she has a contract you signed with Eileen that says you're only here to get me to agree to write a song for her movie. Is that true? Is this all pretend?"

There. He'd asked.

Kenzie froze. Her eyes got big. Her mouth fell open, but she quickly caught herself. She licked at her lips and turned to his mother, who looked as confused as Tucker felt.

"Tell me it's not true," Tucker continued.

Please, God, let her tell him it wasn't true. That Jessica had fucked up.

"There's a contract." Her voice wobbled. "That's true." She wrung her hands together. "Things changed when we got here. When I met everyone. When we talked."

"You never thought to tell me, in all of that, there was an agreement that involved me?" Tucker kept his tone neutral. No emotion.

Emotion could come later.

"I didn't think you'd agree otherwise…" Kenzie glanced around to everyone in the room.

They were all stoic. The Christmas cheer drained from the air.

His family had his back. He knew this. They might've been digging Kenzie, but they had his back. Trust meant everything to a McKay.

His dad said nothing, rolled out of his recliner, headed for the door and grabbed his hat.

The door clicked closed behind him.

Jenny stood. "C'mon, kids. Let's go find the snowmobiles."

She herded her kids to the back door. Her husband, Brian, in tow.

None of them looked at Kenzie.

And Kenzie only looked at Tucker.

"Tucker, c'mon. Things changed. You know things changed."

"I told you no. Twice." Still neutral, he wasn't giving her anything else. He'd already given her everything.

"I just figured once we got some time together you'd see that I need this. That it's important—"

"So you inserted yourself here. With my family."

"Tucker, *you* invited *me*. Coming here was your idea."

Sierra and Cassidy, Brody and Cord all moved toward the back door. None of them said anything. They didn't have to. They knew what was going down. How it was wrecking him.

His mother, however, didn't move. She just stared at Kenzie like Kenzie had kicked her in the stomach.

Tucker could relate.

"We got here and you're singing again," Kenzie continued. "And things between us are good. I figured we could talk about it again later."

"You figured that you'd get under my skin and then I'd say yes."

Fight or flight. And he couldn't fight with her. Not when he felt so much for her.

No, he reminded himself, not her. The woman he'd started to fall for wasn't real. She was a persona Kenzie employed to get her way.

"Tucker..." She started to talk, but he was already heading to the door.

She kept on, "Please don't do thi—"

He closed the door behind him. Headed for his truck.

He'd call Jessica. Have an extraction prepared for Kenzie, so he'd never have to see her again.

13

Chapter Thirteen

"May I use your telephone?" Kenzie used every bit of training she had to keep her shit together.

She'd ruined everything she and Tucker were starting, and her cell was back at the ranch. Too comfortable. She'd gotten too comfortable and let this happen. She'd opened herself up, then the shutters had slammed down and Tucker's feelings had turned frigid—chilling even the fillings in her teeth.

Lori had started to speak a few times, paused, and started again. It was all right though, Kenzie didn't need her sympathy. Kenzie had made this mess. It was hers to wallow in. Lori handed over the phone.

Kenzie punched in Leah's number and waited. "Hi, you've reached Leah. Leave a message."

"Leah, it's Kenzie. I need a pickup." Kenzie paused. Closed her eyes. Took a deep breath. "Please."

Tucking tail and running like she was a thirteen-year-old who had messed up made her head ache.

Leah might not respond for hours. There was only one other person to call. Kenzie dialed, her pulse pounding.

"Hello?" Her mother's voice came through the line.

"Mom?" Kenzie asked. She kept her voice calm. "I'm in Collbran, with Tucker's family. Can you send a car?"

She'd never made a call like this before. Kenzie had never allowed herself to be put in a situation where she'd need to do it.

"Of course," her mother replied, as though they did this all the time. "Are you at Tucker's or…?"

"At his parents' house." Kenzie had no idea where she really was beyond that.

Lori motioned for the phone. Numb, Kenzie handed it to her.

"Hello, this is Tucker's mother… Yes…" She relayed the address. "She's all right. They had a disagreement… Yes… No… She can stay here until someone comes… I don't mind… Yes…you can reach her at this number."

Lori turned off her phone and set it on the arm of the sofa. Her expression was tense.

Kenzie hated, absolutely hated, that she was responsible for that.

"I know we don't know each other well yet," Lori said quietly.

"I'm so sorry I ruined your Christmas," Kenzie replied. An apology wasn't enough, but she had nothing else to give.

Lori shook her head. "Nothing's broken that can't be fixed."

Kenzie sighed. "Tucker probably disagrees."

"Tucker needs some time to figure out how he feels. But for those of us who know him best, we already see he's so far gone for you he'll never come back." Lori set her elbows against her knees, her booted ankle angled to the side. "I think you feel the same way. The looks you two have been giving each other. Those aren't the looks of a Hollywood-brand relationship. They're the real kind."

"I appreciate everything you're saying. I do. Tucker's right, though. I did hope he'd come around and do the song.

It was all about me." She was a spoiled brat, just like her mother always said.

"Well, of course this was all about you. You don't know what it's like to work as part of a team. Not in the family sense."

Kenzie squinted toward her. "I'm not sure I understand—"

"I just spoke with your mother—she's unique—and earlier today I saw how you went from skittish with all the crew to relaxed. After talking with your mama, I can see why. You've never had this before. The craziness of a family that has your back. That's as obvious as the sun rising in the east." Lori took a long breath. "You've always had to look out for yourself. Tucker's always had us. He doesn't know any different. I didn't always have a family like this. So, I built one. I think you'll do the same. And if Tucker gets his head screwed on right again, he'll see that he wants it to be with him."

Lori's phone buzzed on the armrest. She didn't even glance at it before she handed it to Kenzie. "Everyone I know is here."

Kenzie glanced at the Caller ID.

Leah.

"Hello?" Kenzie asked.

"I've got a car headed your way. Already coordinated with your mother. Tucker's manager connected, too. That's who I was talking with when you called."

Kenzie swallowed the cotton that had taken up residence in her throat. Tucker wanted her gone bad enough he'd called his manager.

There'd be no working any of this out.

"The car will take you to your mother's condo in Vail. I'm getting a charter flight there now. We can figure out the rest this afternoon."

Kenzie looked to Lori.

Lori was wrong.

Leah had her back, Tucker wasn't coming around, and Kenzie wouldn't open herself up to someone again.

"That'd be great," she heard herself say the words, but inside she felt numb.

Numb was better than pain. Numb was a good place to be.

A weight had fallen on her life, like the winter storm dumping a foot of snow on the mountains. The difference was, for her, the weight wouldn't melt away when spring came.

Her career was probably over. She wasn't coming back from the last box office disaster. The man she'd started to fall for would likely never speak to her again.

She'd made an epic mess of things.

And now, it was time to figure out what came next.

TUCKER HAD GONE FOR A DRIVE. The back road, country Christmas kind—long and winding. And it did nothing to clear his head.

He pulled up to the ranch.

His father sat in one of the rocking chairs Jenny had placed outside the door, whittling a piece of wood. The pile of shavings at his boots said he'd been at it awhile.

"Where in the hell have you been?" he asked, not looking up from the knife and the hunk of pine.

"Getting away. Same as you." Tucker dropped to the other rocking chair.

Dad whistled out a breath. "Boy, you are an idiot."

"Say what?"

"Thought you were smarter than this."

"I didn't know what she was up to."

"Not that. The letting *that* determine your future. She was taking care of herself. That's all she's ever known."

"I don't think you understand the ramifications of what she tried to get me roped into."

"Would it have ended with you two together?"

"Maybe."

"Then I don't figure the rest matters." A thick wood shaving fell at their feet.

"She lied to me."

His father kept his focus on the wood, smoothing a bit with the pad of his thumb. "When you asked her if she did it, the girl didn't hedge. She admitted it and tried to explain."

"You left first," Tucker pointed out.

Another deep sigh. "I left so everyone else would leave, so you two could talk. Not so you could take off to God knows where for two hours. The girl loves you. You love her. Both of you are too hardheaded to see it, but that's how it is."

Did he love her? Could a guy fall in love with a girl in the short amount of time they'd been together?

Maybe?

Holy shit. He did.

Sonofabitch.

"She doesn't have what you have in a family. She only has herself. Are you going to let it stay that way?" Dad asked.

No, he wasn't. "I'll go talk to her. Is she still with Mom?"

"No. She left. An hour ago. While you were out lollygagging around, a car came and picked her up."

Tucker's throat felt covered in grit, his heart a weight in his chest holding him down. "I've got to find her."

"First you've got to get her a decent Christmas present."

Yes, yes he did.

And he knew just what to do.

DARKNESS HAD ALREADY FALLEN when Tucker pulled up to the condo in Vail. Kenzie's mother was having her annual Christmas party. Tucker hoped his invitation was still valid.

He'd had Jessica find out where Kenzie had gone.

He'd spent the day perfecting Kenzie's song. Driven two hours. And he was here.

To win her back.

It was below freezing, but Tucker was sweating.

Now was the time.

He stepped from the truck, his cowboy boots seeping into the slush. The valet took his name. Checked over the list. Then he took Tucker's keys.

Tucker climbed the steps to the building like a man scaling a mountain. Slow and steady. One step at a time.

The butler opened the door and the party was in full swing. Champagne flowed while tuxedo-wearing waiters swirled through the room and Christmas music played.

He spotted Kenzie by a window talking to her manager, a glass of what he knew was untouched seltzer water in her hand. His heart tried to stop beating at the sight of her. He liked her polished up like this, but he liked her better with messy hair he'd mussed himself. Right now, he'd take her however she'd give herself to him.

He tipped the hired piano player two hundred dollars to take a break. Then Tucker sat at the keyboard, the thin sheen of sweat no longer just a sheen.

His fingers found the keys, he closed his eyes, lifted his lips to the microphone, and he sang for Kenzie.

Her song. The one he'd written for her that day.

Her Christmas present.

The room went quiet, as he'd known it would. Tucker McKay singing at a Christmas party didn't happen.

This wasn't for them, though. This was for Kenzie.

He put everything he had into the music.

When the final chord played, he finished with, "I wrote this for Mackenzie Bennett. It's her song. Merry Christmas."

He opened his eyes. Kenzie stood at the end of the piano, her expression gentle. She moved to where he sat. He didn't move, afraid she'd get skittish and disappear. He'd lived through that once. There was no way he could do it twice.

"You're here," she said, as though trying to believe it herself.

He turned off the microphone and pushed it away so their conversation would be private. "I couldn't just let you leave. Not after everything."

"I didn't think you wanted me home with you anymore."

He wanted to touch her, but he hadn't earned that right. Not yet. "Kenzie, you're my home. Wherever you are, that's my home."

She bit at her lower lip, her eyes misting.

"The song is yours to do with whatever you want. Give it to Eileen, whatever you want. It's yours."

"Leah let Eileen know I'm not doing the movie. This afternoon, she made a few calls." Kenzie set her seltzer water on a coaster by the microphone. "I'm not going to let someone like that decide my career for me."

"The song is still yours."

"I…I'm going to produce my own screenplay. I thought about what you said. I want to do this, but I want to do it myself. Be in charge for once."

"Then I'll be there for you. With whatever you need." Pride radiated through him. She was taking control of her destiny.

"I just need you, Tucker." Her voice cracked on his name.

That's when he stood, ran his hand through her hair, and kissed her.

And she kissed him right back.

Epilogue
FOUR YEARS, THREE MONTHS LATER...

The limousine crept to the red carpet outside the Dolby Theatre. Kenzie looked to Tucker. He stared out the window, elbow on the armrest attached to the door, his fingertip tapping against his chin.

They'd been married for years. And they loved each other more now than the day they'd said their vows.

"Tucker will go first. Then me. Then Clint. Then you." Kenzie squeezed Lori's hand. "It's loud and there are a lot of cameras. If it gets to be too much, tell Tucker. He'll hurry you through."

They'd already rehearsed everything, from the limousine exit to the best way to walk the carpet outside the industry's biggest award show.

Lori still hadn't taken a breath.

"Breathe or you're going to pass out," Clint said to his wife.

Lori sucked in a deep breath.

"Keep doin' that." Clint went back to staring out the other window.

He sat next to Tucker. Kenzie sat with Lori.

Kenzie had invited her own mother, but she was on a two-month African safari with her now husband. They'd met the night Tucker sang Kenzie her song.

She was happy, which made Kenzie happy.

Tucker looked over at her and butterflies flitted through her belly. He still managed to do that, even after all the time they'd been together.

She ran a hand over the satin dress at her waist. Her baby bump was more than visible now. This would be their first time officially acknowledging she was pregnant. They'd wanted to keep it to themselves as long as possible.

She glanced to her belly. It wasn't possible anymore.

"Dear lord, don't let me trip," Lori said under her breath.

"Take it from my experience, falling face-first publicly isn't the worst thing that could happen." Kenzie held Tucker's gaze. A whisper of a grin played at the edge of his mouth. "Actually, I think it's probably the best thing that ever happened to me," Kenzie continued.

She got the guy. He gave her a family. And now her screenplay was up for Best Picture. The little production company she had started with Tucker wasn't so little anymore. They were about to have a really big night.

The limousine came to a stop. The chauffer opened the door. Tucker slid out. Kenzie scooted over to go next. She needed a little extra help to get out, so he shielded her from the click beetles with his body until she was camera ready.

Kenzie reached for his hand and traced the line of the gold band she'd put there. Positioned for the cameras, he moved aside and gave her hand a little squeeze.

Like they were the real deal.

Because they were.

Stay in Touch

Sign up for Christina's newsletter here:
ChristinaHovland.com/newsletter

Acknowledgments

Thanks to my husband, Steve, and four kids for being patient while I wrote and edited this story over summer break. I couldn't follow my dream without the support of each of you.

Thanks to my mother, Shirley, and sister, Sereneti, for cheering me on.

To Tres and Erika for being there to support me.

And to my dad, who was a lot of the inspiration for Tucker's dad and his many dad-isms. I wish you were here to see this. I miss you.

The Lyons Clan from Collbran (and everywhere else). I'm so blessed to be part of this family.

My best friend, Karie, for always being there for me. Literally, always being there for me. I adore you.

Kiele, for being my person even when I get a little neurotic, and for being the voice of reason when I need one.

L.A. Mitchell, the best writing coach an author could ask for. I'm so grateful for you.

My first-line readers on this story: A.Y. Chao, Christine Grissom, Jody Holford, Diane Holiday, and Dylann Crush.

My agent, Emily Sylvan Kim, for helping to move my production schedule around so this story could be possible.

Holly Ingraham for being such an awesome editor. I just love working with you.

Thank you, Laura, for the care you took with this manuscript in its final stages. I am so appreciative of your professionalism.

The Rebelles for your constant support.

And, as always, the Romance Chicks: Renee, Jody & Dylann.

Also by Christina Hovland

The Mile High Matched Series

Rock Hard Cowboy

Going Down on One Knee

Blow Me Away

Take It Off the Menu

Do Me a Favor

Ball Sacked

The Mile High Rocked Series

Played by the Rockstar

From Entangled Publishing

The Honeymoon Trap

Rachel, Out of Office

April May Fall

About the Author

Christina Hovland lives her own version of a fairy tale—an artisan chocolatier by day and romance writer by night. Born in Colorado, Christina received a degree in journalism from Colorado State University. Before opening her chocolate company, Christina's career spanned from the television newsroom to managing an award-winning public relations firm. She's a recovering overachiever and perfectionist with a love of cupcakes and dinner she doesn't have to cook herself. A 2017 Golden Heart® finalist, she lives in Colorado with her first-boyfriend-turned-husband, four children, and the sweetest dogs around.

ChristinaHovland.com

facebook.com/HovlandWrites

twitter.com/HovlandWrites

instagram.com/HovlandWrites

goodreads.com/HovlandWrites

bookbub.com/profile/christina-hovland

**Turn the page for chapter one of
Going Down on One Knee**

**He's a Rocker. He's a Biker. He's the wedding
planner.**

Number-crunching Velma Johnson's perfectly planned life is right on course.

That's a lie. Sure, she's got the lucrative job. She's got the posh apartment. But her sister nabbed Velma's Mr. Right. There has to be a man out there for Velma. Hopefully, one who's hunky, wears pressed suits, and has a diversified financial portfolio. He'll be exactly like, well... her sister's new fiancé.

Badass biker Brek Montgomery blazes a trail across the country, managing Dimefront, one of the biggest rock bands of his generation. With the band on hiatus, Brek rolls into Denver to pay a quick visit to his family and friends. But when Brek's sister suddenly gets put on bed rest, she convinces Brek to take over her wedding planning business for the duration of her pregnancy.

Staying in Denver and dealing with bridezillas was not what Brek had in mind when he passed through town, but there is one particular maid-of-honor who might make his stay worthwhile.

Velma finds herself strangely attracted to the man planning her sister's wedding. Problem is, he ticks none of the boxes on her well-crafted list. Brek is rough around the edges, he cusses, and doesn't even have a 401(k). But trying something crazy might get her out of the rut of her dating life--so long as she lays down boundaries up front and sticks to her plan...

Chapter One
THE COUNTDOWN BEGINS

Three words. Three. Little. Words. Nothing important.

Okay, so the three words were important. Massive, really.

"Congratulations, you two," Velma Johnson rehearsed aloud to the vase of a dozen yellow roses gripped in her arms. With a reaffirming gulp of Denver's crisp spring air, she hustled through the open-air parking garage to the security door of her apartment building.

Her sister, Claire, had big news. To be exact, Claire and her boyfriend, Dean, had big news. Velma had a feeling she knew exactly what their news would be—they were moving in together. The next step in their relationship. Tension in Velma's neck strung tight at the thought.

A successful career and a posh apartment she could eventually rent out as an investment were steps one and two of Velma's elaborate five-year plan. She had ticked both those boxes. Dean, three kids, and moving to a two-story house just outside of Denver had been steps three through seven.

Not anymore. Now, her sister was moving in with the man Velma had crushed on for years. The one Velma measured all others against. The one she sang Prince and Madonna songs with at the office.

Yes, they were moving in together. That's why Claire had called yesterday and asked to take her to dinner. Velma had insisted they meet at her place instead. Her invitation had nothing to do with the fact she liked having Dean visit her apartment—even if he was with her sister. She'd offered because it made sense they'd want a private location for their big reveal. And when the announcement came that they'd be embracing that next relationship milestone…well, being on her home turf sounded pretty darn appealing.

Just as she reached the security door, the sound of a motorcycle that clearly had no muffler cut through her thoughts. She turned. The bike pulled up next to her car—into the parking spot meant for her guests. A super-muscled, badass-mother-trucker of a biker swung his leg over the side of the motorcycle and stood.

Her heart stopped with a *thunk*.

Vin-Diesel-biker-dude pulled off his helmet and—sweet mother of Mary, had the temperature jumped by ten degrees? She got the picture: he rode a motorcycle, hit the gym twice a day. The type she avoided because she did not do badass. She preferred the suspenders-and-slacks kind of man. Except, at that moment, she debated how important that preference really was to her.

Focus, Velma. Head held high, she approached him. "Excuse me? Sir? You can't park there."

He frowned at the number marking the spot.

Normally she wouldn't mind sharing the space, but with Claire, Dean, and his friend Brek coming to dinner, she needed both of her parking spaces.

This man was obviously not Dean's friend. Dean's friends were all buttoned-up, suit-wearing, Wednesday-afternoon golfers. She was nearly certain.

The black leather jacket and jeans ripped at this guy's knees looked horribly out of place next to her Prius. His longish, rock-'n'-roll blond hair was nicer than hers (although his could use a trim). She didn't even mind the dragon tattoo creeping around the side of his neck or the layer of mud coating his motorcycle boots. Everything about the man screamed masculine.

Velma shifted the heavy vase in her grip. *Fudge.* Which of her neighbors was letting their guests use her spot this time?

"No, see, that's the spot for my apartment." Oh, how she wanted to rub at the headache pulsing at her forehead. She didn't have time for this. Not today. "I'm sorry, it's just that my sister and her boyfriend and his friend are coming for dinner because my sister has big news. And while I have no idea what that news is, it's important to her. So that makes it important to me. Which is why I put on a pork roast, bought roses, and got out my crystal wine goblets. That's what you do when your sister has big news, you know? Never mind she's practically living my five-year plan without even trying, and I'm over here without even a boyfriend. *That* was not part of my plan. At this point, I should be at least six months into dating my future husband."

Oh God. She was rambling. And he was staring at her with a half grin that made her skin flush. Seriously, the way the man smiled should be outlawed.

She ducked her head. "Anyway, I have company coming and I kind of need my spot."

"Five-year plan?" he asked. As though that was the important part of what she'd just spit out.

This is how one makes an absolute idiot of oneself. "You know what? It's fine. You can stay right there. Don't worry about it." She shifted the flowers again and turned on her heel.

See? People said she was inflexible, but here she was, absolutely rolling with it. She smiled at her flexibility.

"One sec," Motorcycle Dude called. "This is the number they gave me."

She paused midstride and turned around.

He ticked his head to the side. "Velvet?"

Oh dear. She could easily be swayed by the gravelly way he said her name. Well, the nickname her family called her—despite her repeated cease-and-desist requests.

"Um, yes?" She gripped the glass vase harder with her clammy hands.

"Brek." He looked at her like she should know him and pointed to his chest. "Dean's friend."

Velma stared.

Oh.

This was Brek? She'd expected him to wear khaki pants and drive a Camry. He reached into one of his saddlebags and held up a six-pack of Coors and a four-pack of Bartles & Jaymes fuzzy-navel-flavored wine coolers. "Claire asked me to bring the beer and wine, since I'm crashing your party."

Wine coolers? She stared some more. *Be flexible,* she reminded herself. *Flexible. Flexible. Flexible.*

"Great. Fuzzy navel pairs perfectly with pork roast." Cheeks burning and arms full, she managed to open the security door.

"So, you're Claire's sister?" His lazy gaze trailed over her.

"The one and only."

His deep-blue eyes rivaled the color of the razzleberry lollipops she loved. The kind that made her mouth water just thinking about them and… *Focus, Velma.*

"Can I come up, Velvet?" His deep voice held a subtle hint of roughness.

"Velma," she corrected. "You're a little early. I'm so behind. Normally, I'm much more together."

"I can come back later." Brek's eyes softened, totally contrary to his outer badassery.

"No. I am officially the queen of flexibility. It's not a problem."

He did the darn grin thing again. She silently instructed her body to ignore it.

"Queen of flexibility. That ought to be interesting," he

mumbled mostly to himself but loud enough for her to hear. He stepped next to her, balanced the beer and "wine" against the impressive muscles of one arm, and slid the vase she carried into the crook of his other arm.

"Thanks." This time it was her turn to mumble.

Without looking back, she led him up the stairs to her apartment. Another glance his way, and she'd probably trip face-first into the wall or something equally embarrassing. To prevent herself from taking another peek, she focused on sticking the key in the keyhole of her apartment door as though it took every ounce of her concentration.

There. The door swung open. He stepped through the doorframe, close enough for her to catch the scent of leather and Irish Spring soap. Close enough for her to reach out and touch the stubble running over his jawline. Close enough for her to—she shook her head to dislodge the abrupt light-headedness.

"This place is huge." With a long whistle, he set every-thing down on her dining room table.

Vaulted ceilings, open concept, white walls and sofa, with pops of jewel tones in her carefully selected décor; it must all appear so unnecessary to a guy like him. But these were her things, proof of everything she had worked so hard to achieve.

Brek walked into the kitchen and glanced to the slow cooker on the counter. "This smells amazing, Velvet. You a chef?"

"Velma," she corrected him again, slipping on an apron with the words *Domestic Diva* embroidered on the front. "And no, I just like to cook."

Velma took in the dinner she'd spent the afternoon plan-ning and preparing. Vegetables had been roasted in the oven, and a chocolate cream pie was setting in the fridge. Not the pudding kind, either. A real, honest-to-goodness, made-from-whipping-cream-and-two-kinds-of-chocolate pie. She hoped she could eat those leftovers while she binge-watched Rodgers and Hammerstein musicals later.

"Then what do you do, Vel*ma*?" His emphasis on the last syllable made her wish her name wasn't so frumpy.

"For employment?" she asked.

"Yeah…or pleasure."

The expression on his face and the way he drew out the word "pleasure" made her toes curl in her sandals.

Right, employment. He'd asked about her work.

"I'm a financial planner," she replied.

Brek rubbed his hands together. "Like Dean?"

"Yup." She and Dean had worked together for years. "Our offices are across the hall from each other. That's how Dean met Claire." Claire had come to visit Velma at work and had wandered into Dean's office by accident.

That was the day Velma's dream of becoming Mrs. Dean Stuart died—all because she had waited too long to make her move and lost her chance.

Mr. Right had met her sister and they'd ended up together, making kissy faces during Thanksgiving dinner.

Actually, they never made kissy faces. The two of them were much too classy for that.

Brek leaned his hip against her granite countertop and crossed his leather-covered arms. "No idea what Dean does at his job, either, but I'm sure you're both fantastic at it."

"We help people with their financial portfolios. Annuities, estate plans, investment management, things like that. What about you?"

"I'm in the music industry." He snagged one of the crystal wine goblets she'd put out earlier and swaggered toward her.

Her stomach did a loop the loop. The swagger affected her more than expected. "You play in a band?"

"Nah. I play guitar, but not professionally. I manage a band." He popped the top off a wine cooler and poured it all the way to the tippy top of the glass. Then he edged inside her personal-space bubble and handed her the glass.

"Thanks." Normally, she didn't drink much—especially on Sundays. Monday marked the start of the week, with new chances and opportunities. She preferred to start it at her best, not hung over with a headache.

Then again, tonight was the night of change. Big-news change. My-sister's-moving-in-with-my-dream-man change. So Velma would have a wine cooler—no use in wasting it when Brek had already poured it—and ignore her attraction to Dean. Steps to a new life filled with…finding a new man who was as perfect for her as Dean was. Baby steps and all that.

Brek slipped off his jacket and tossed it over one of the island barstools. Tattoos ran from the short sleeves of his black T-shirt to his wrists. They looked tribal, mostly wild, and super-hot. If one liked tattoos. Which, she reminded herself, she did not.

"Claire says you two are twins?" Brek asked.

"Uh-huh," she muttered around a gulp of carbonated peach drink.

"You and Claire don't look like twins," Brek said.

Velma pulled a stack of small, hand-painted dessert plates from her for-company-only dish cupboard. "We're not identical."

"No kidding," he replied, serious. "It's the eyes."

Ha. Hardly just the eyes. Velma's eyes were muted gray, like a painter had finished painting for the day and just didn't feel like adding more cyan to the palette. Claire's were a rich brown. More than that, Claire was thin and Velma, well…she was Velma. All curves, like her mother. No matter how many calories she counted or steps the app on her phone registered, the curves stayed put. Velma's hair was dirty blonde. Not the attractive kind, either. In-desperate-need-of-highlights blonde was more like it. Claire's hair was a beautiful deep-chestnut color.

"Why does Claire call you Velvet?" Brek asked.

She sighed and paused, plate in hand. "Family nickname. No matter how many times I ask them to stop."

"Velma." He seemed to be testing the name, letting it melt on his tongue like warm chocolate on a vanilla sundae.

"Not a name I'd lie about." She set out the last of the plates on the table.

"I like it. It's original." The low, rumbly words made her lungs constrict in a warm way she refused to acknowledge.

"Unfortunately, it's not even original." She pulled a cutting board from the pantry. "Claire was born first, so she got the cool name. I was born three minutes later and got Velma."

"It's an interesting name."

"Velma was my grandmother's name. But there couldn't be two of us in the same family, so they all call me Velvet."

"I like Velvet," he said.

She scrunched up her nose. "I don't."

When she was a child, everyone bought her clothes with cheap velvet fabric. They itched. She hated them. As far as she was concerned, velvet was scratchy and uncomfortable.

"This news. Any idea what it is?" Velma asked.

"You don't know?" Brek replied.

"No idea." Except she was absolutely certain they were taking the next step in their relationship by moving in together, and maybe getting a puppy.

Brek popped the top on a Coors. "I figured you and Claire shared everything."

"Nope." Not this time. "Claire just said she has big news."

"Maybe she's knocked up," Brek suggested.

Velma's heart skipped five beats. She grabbed a knife and sliced into an onion with renewed energy. "No way."

"I don't know." He ran a palm over the back of his neck. "Seems reasonable to me."

"Then you don't know Claire. She's way too involved in her career to get pregnant right now." Velma set the onions aside and went to work on chopping carrots to top the salad.

Brek motioned to the cutting board. "Can I help you with anything?"

"Do you know how to julienne carrots?" Velma replied.

"Nope." He shrugged. "But I know how to cook a steak."

She laughed. "Well, tonight it's pork roast, so I'll have to take a rain check on your culinary skills."

"Absolutely. Next time I'm in town, I'll grill you up a steak." He raised his beer to her.

She stared at him. He couldn't actually be serious.

He was serious.

"Maybe they called us here because Dean needs a kidney?" he asked.

"He doesn't need a kidney." Although, Velma would probably give him one if needed. She had a remarkably hard time telling him no. "They're probably just…" *Say it out loud, Velma.* She sighed. "Just moving in together."

"Nah. They wouldn't have dragged me here for that. Maybe their big news is they're gonna try to hook us up."

"You and me?" Velma pointed the knife at Brek, then back to herself.

Of all the options, that one was the most reasonable. And, yet, totally unreasonable. No way would Claire pair the two of them together.

"You said you don't have a guy." Brek's tone turned serious.

Her body irrationally responded to his apparent interest with tingles.

"No." Of course she didn't have a guy.

She'd had lots of first dates lately.

"I get the feeling you need some help loosening up. Enjoy

some time away from your five-year-husband-seeking plan. There's a club downtown with a great band playing later. We should go." Brek's gaze raked over her.

His pointed interest was actually…nice. Still, there was no way she would go clubbing later. Brek wasn't her type. Not only because of the tattoos or the extreme need for a licensed barber or his ripped jeans. No, it was more the general sense of unease he stirred within her. Also, it was Sunday. What kind of a club was open on a Sunday night? Definitely not one she should visit.

"You stressed about the dinner?" he asked.

"No," she lied through her teeth.

"You're stressed about the dinner," he declared. "I get that, but there's nothing to worry about."

For a half second, she believed there was nothing to worry about. Truth was, there was always something to worry about. Starting with her clothes. She needed to change into something that wasn't yoga pants before her sister arrived in what would undoubtedly be a perfect sundress.

"I'm only in town for a few days anyway," he continued. "We'll get through the part where Claire and Dean do the awkward you-two-should-get-to-know-each-other schtick. We'll eat and then we'll send them on their way. You don't want to go to a club? That's fine. I'll stick around. What do you say, Velma?"

The way he said her name felt like silk against her skin. Silk was so much nicer than velvet.

She tried to tug off her apron, but her hair was stuck in the tie at the back of her neck. Crud. Another tug. Her hair was really stuck. "You want to go clubbing on a Sunday night?"

"Absolutely." He nodded to where her hair was caught. "Need some help?"

"Yes, please." She pressed her eyes closed.

He looped a finger under the little bow tying the apron at

the back of her neck. His calloused fingertip traced the ribbon along her shoulder to the collar of her sweater, unraveling the knot of hair and sending little shivers along his path of exploration.

Maybe she could get away to the club for a little while. It wasn't like she had better things to do. "Where is this cl—"

"Hey, Velvet." Her sister, Claire, shoved open the front door. "Hi, Brek. You made it. Dean's so excited you're here."

"Did you lose him?" Brek squeezed Velma's shoulder.

A hit of sizzle deep in her belly echoed the motion of his touch.

"He's parking the car." Claire closed the door and sauntered to the kitchen with her svelte build and Audrey Hepburn grace. "Okay, I know I've made you wait. But…" Claire bit at the light-pink lipstick on her bottom lip. "Surprise!" She held out her fingers with a little jazz hand motion.

An *engagement* ring perched on the fourth finger of Claire's left hand.

Velma's heart skidded to her toes. She blinked hard. No, it couldn't be.

A ring.

A wedding.

Satin and lace, champagne toasts and flower girls.

This wasn't a puppy. And it was so much more than an apartment.

Velma reached for Claire's hand, her throat constricting. "Oh my gosh."

"I know, right?" Claire squeezed Velma's fingers. "I had to tell you in person."

"Oh. My. Gosh." Velma said again, this time more slowly. She looked straight into Claire's eyes and saw it—excitement and love for Dean. Happiness. Velma glued a grin onto her face. Her sister was happy. That was all that mattered. "Claire. It's perfect."

"I'm gonna go find Dean." Brek caught Velma's gaze and winked. "Now that the cat's out of the bag."

"Wait, you knew about this?" Velma asked.

"Hell yeah, I knew." Brek opened the door. "Didn't want to ruin Claire's surprise, though."

"So you asked me out instead?" Velma asked.

Claire scrunched up her forehead. "Brek asked you out? Like on a date?"

"Oh look, it's Dean." Brek feigned innocence as he held the door wide. "I'm officially saved by the groom."

"She finally told her?" Dean strode inside and glanced to where Velma stood in a swirling vortex of time.

"Uh-huh." Claire nodded, her eyes misted over.

A suit. Dean wore a tailored suit complete with shined cap-toed shoes and gold cuff links. Each black hair on his head lay precisely where it should. He was absolute perfection.

Velma swallowed the heaviness in her throat and tried to pretend it was from excitement for her sister.

"Well, then—hey, sis." Dean strutted toward Velma and wrapped her in a hug. "Claire made me keep my mouth shut for a whole week."

Velma's insides did a little flutter that was totally unacceptable. Time moved at the speed of a sloth. Like watching a car accident happen in real time, when everything went slow and then fast again all at once. "You've been engaged for a week and didn't say anything?"

They'd sat through a load of sales meetings. Two client lunches where he'd driven them both to the restaurant. He'd never given any indication he'd freaking proposed to her sister. They'd discussed retirement plans and supplemental income sources. He hadn't mentioned anything that would've even whispered of proposal news.

"Believe me, it was hard keeping my mouth shut. Can you

believe you're going to be my little sister?" His breath brushed against the top of her head.

"Uh…nope," Velma said through gritted teeth.

"It's great, isn't it?" Dean leaned back and scanned her face.

Her knees went weak, like a cheesy movie heroine.

"It is great. Totally. Great. I'm so excited." Velma stepped away from him, refusing to show anything but happiness for her sister's sake. Any feelings from now on would be purely of the appropriate sisterly kind.

Claire and Dean were engaged.

Yup, Velma's Mr. Right was going to marry her sister.

Enjoyed the sample?
Going Down on One Knee is available now!

Going Down on One Knee
Copyright ©2018 Christina Hovland
All rights reserved